THE UGLY ONE

THE UGLY ONE

by Leanne Statland Ellis

Clarion Books
Houghton Mifflin Harcourt
Boston • New York

Clarion Books
215 Park Avenue South
New York, New York 10003

Clarion Books is an imprint of Houghton Mifflin Harcourt Publishing Company.

www.hmhbooks.com

The text was set in 13-point Chaparral.
Book design by Kerry Martin

Library of Congress Cataloging-in-Publication Data
Ellis, Leanne Statland.
The Ugly One / by Leanne Statland Ellis.
p. cm.
Summary: At the height of the Incan empire, a girl called the Ugly One
because of a disfiguring scar on her face seeks to have the scar removed
and instead finds a life path as a shaman. —Provided by publisher
ISBN 978-0-547-64023-5 (hardcover : alk. paper)
[1. Disfigured persons—Fiction. 2. Beauty, Personal—Fiction. 3. Self-esteem—Fiction.
4. Incas—Fiction. 5. Indians of South America—Peru—Fiction. 6. Shamans—Fiction.
7. Fate and fatalism—Fiction. 8. Peru—History—To 1548—Fiction.] I. Title.
PZ7.E4738Ugl 2013
[Fic]—dc23
2012017182

Manufactured in the United States of America
DOC 10 9 8 7 6 5 4 3 2 1
4500411296

With much gratitude to my family for their support and encouragement during the writing of this book, to Marcia Leonard for brilliantly guiding it to its final shape with such care, and to Dinah Stevenson for welcoming it to Clarion Books.

· · · · · · · · · · · · · · · · ·

For girls everywhere—

may each and every one of you discover

your power, your voice, and your beauty.

And for my girl, Layla Dawn,

whose inner and outer beauty shine so brightly.

. . . .

I love this girl like the sun loves to shine.

I said, I love this girl like the sun loves to shine.

I love to hug her and kiss her,

this beautiful daughter of mine.

–L.S.E.

ÑAWPA PACHAPI
· ·
Once Upon a Time

Ñawpa pachapi, once upon a time, when I was a young girl, my favorite thing to do was sit on the outskirts of the fire circle and listen to one of my Uncle Turu's stories. His words would take hold of me and lift me far away, to the sacred mountains and the hot jungles and the first conversations our ancestors had with the sun. I needed his stories, for the times when he told them were the only times I truly forgot myself, forgot how hideously ugly I was.

And now I find that I, too, can be a storyteller. My words are worth listening to, I think, and there is some wisdom in them. Now that I am no longer the Ugly One.

It all began the day the jungle stranger came to our village and changed my path with a gift. I was twelve, sitting on my rock alone, as was my way, when he first arrived. Of course, my story truly began years before that day, but I will start here for now, for many good stories begin with the day when a life changes. Any storyteller worth listening to knows this is so.

1
MILLAY
Ugly One

THE sun flashed behind the *molle* leaves, turning them a brilliant green. They were cut into long, thin segments by the dark hair that always sat like a shield in front of my right eye. I had been ugly as far back as I could remember. "Millay, Ugly One," they said, "cover your face." Or "Loathsome One, turn toward the mountain — it is more forgiving." I watched the world through the protective strands of my hair.

As I shifted my weight on the unyielding stone, a few hairs caught in my eyelashes. I brushed them away and turned my attention back to the soft white alpaca wool resting on my lap. Slowly, I worked my hands through it, picking out tiny burrs and dust flecks so that it would be clean for Mama to spin. It was from one of the young animals. Their wool was the softest, the most desirable. I lifted a cleaned clump and lightly rubbed it against my smooth left cheek, up and down, side to side. In a deliberate arc, I moved it across my forehead. When it touched my right eyebrow, I slowed, using it to trace the deep scar that ran like a river from my right eye down my cheek to my lip and lowered my mouth in a permanent half frown. I used to believe that if I rubbed the alpaca hard enough into my skin, it would make the scar smooth and soft. Of course this did not happen, but I still enjoyed the feeling on my face.

"Micay?" a voice called from below.

It was Chasca, my older sister. She was the only one who called me by my given name. Mama and Papa called me Daughter. My older brother, Hatun, called me Sister. To the others, I was always Millay, Ugly One.

"Are you up there, sitting on your rock?" Chasca called, although she already knew the answer to this question. No one but my sister climbed this steep path to find me. Her dark head appeared, followed by the rest of her body. She smiled as she sighted me, her face smooth and beautiful. Chasca, Morning Star. It was as if my parents had known, when they named her as a newborn, how brightly her smile would shine. Cupping her hands around her mouth, she shouted up, "A visitor has come!"

This was a surprise. People rarely came to our village. It was small, only sixty people who were more likely to leave than bring others, and it was difficult to find, tucked high up in the mountains.

"Who has come?" I asked.

"He says he is from the *yunka*."

From the jungle? I could feel my eyes grow wide. We had heard stories of the faraway land below the mountains where the air was always hot and thick with water. But I had never met anyone who had been there.

"He has brought things I think you will like," Chasca added. She turned back to the village and beckoned for me to follow. I hesitated. I preferred to be alone, but the lure of the *yunka* stranger was too strong. I stood, placing the alpaca wool in a basket at my hip. Then, careful to rest my hair over my right cheek, I headed down the slope.

❖❖

The stranger was surrounded by the people. His hair was different — shorter than the custom in the mountains. It looked as if he had placed a bowl on his head and cut off that which hung below the rim. And he wore a small piece of wood stuck through the skin at the bottom of his nose. Spread out around him were the many objects that he had brought to trade. Among them I recognized the weavings of some of the nearby villages. He must have traded for these things on his way here. There were also bundles of colorful feathers, spotted furs, exotic fruits, dead butterflies of unusual color and size, and pouches of what I guessed to be jungle herbs. The people were touching and pointing and shouting, excited by the strange objects from so far away.

Uncle Turu, Mama's brother, was waving his arms about in front of the *yunka* stranger. He was a large and loud man, my uncle, and he yelled and pointed at a cluster of long red feathers, the kind used to weave fine capes for the royalty and priests of the cities. Uncle Turu was trying to intimidate the stranger into a trade, pushing his nose close to the man's face, snorting like the turu, the bull for which he was named. It is strange the way a name can shape a person. I watched my uncle, already knowing his tactics wouldn't work. Uncle Turu was a storyteller who liked to fling his arms about for show, but inside he was as soft as the baby alpaca's fleece. He didn't like to take advantage of travelers who came to trade. I was sure the stranger would make the better deal before these two were done.

I pulled my right hand through my hair and stepped closer to the large, noisy crowd, hoping no one would notice me in the commotion.

A small group of boys huddled in a circle off to the side, laughing and sneering. I usually stayed away from these boys. But something about the way they moved, their bodies all scrunched over and their attention focused, made me want to see what they were looking at.

Ucho, their leader, was only a year older than me, but he was much bigger. He bent to pick up a stick, and I saw that there was a very small animal in the center of these boys. Ucho poked at it to show his courage to the others. Each time he jabbed he made a strange animal sound, "Kee! Kee! Kee!" Then the others all laughed and imitated him. "Kee! Kee!"

The tiny creature didn't move, and I couldn't tell if it was alive or dead. I wanted to scream and rush in and stomp on them like they were little ants. Instead, I squeezed my hands into fists and stayed where I was, watching through my layer of hair.

Suddenly, Muti, Ucho's six-year-old brother, spied me. At once he was pointing and screeching, "Kee! Kee! Look, the Ugly One is here. Millay shows her face."

I turned to leave, but the boys rushed around me in a circle, blocking the way. Ucho still had his stick, and he poked it at my side — not hard, but also not gently. He squawked, "Millay! Millay! Go back to the rocks. Keekeekee!"

I would like to say that I was used to such words, that they didn't bother me, but they did. They hurt me deeply. I shouldn't have come. I should have stayed safely on my rock.

Ucho lifted the stick higher and tried to move my hair away from my face. I dropped my basket and covered the scar with my hands, holding the skin tightly. I could not escape, so I looked to the sky, to Inti, the beautiful sun, trying to lose myself in his glowing golden warmth. The stick was in my side again, poking for my attention, but still I looked up, ignoring the ugly shouts. The clouds soared above, changing their shape, their size, as they passed by. I thought, *What power they have, to move like this. If I had such power, I would use it right now to soar up to beautiful Inti and never come back.*

The stick was gone. I dared to look down and saw the *yunka* stranger holding Ucho by the neck, lifting him off the ground with one hand. The man scowled as he studied Ucho, as if the boy were smeared in fresh llama dung that was unpleasant to the nose. Ucho glared back at the man, but his body showed that he was frightened.

The other boys scattered like little rabbits. This was my opportunity to run to safety, but before my feet could turn, the stranger grabbed my shoulder tightly with his other hand. I struggled to free myself, but his powerful grip held me firmly in place. My chest pounded in fear. I forced myself to look into his face and to keep my body stiff to hide my fright. His eyes studied me intently—deep brown eyes that I didn't understand—but at least he didn't dangle me off the ground like a dead animal or look at me as if I smelled unpleasant.

The *yunka* man turned his head back to Ucho and threw the boy to the ground. Dust flew up in a cloud, and Ucho coughed. He didn't rise, and I wondered if he was hurt or shamed. I hoped both. The man pointed to the small animal on the ground. Then in broken speech, for he was a stranger to our language, he commanded, "Bring Sumac Huanacauri to me!"

Sumac Huanacauri. Handsome Rainbow. This was a mighty name for so tiny a creature, and there were smiles in the crowd. But no one made a sound.

Slowly, Ucho rose, careful to look at no one. He raised his shoulders pridefully and walked to the little animal still lying on the ground. Scooping it into his hands, he delivered the pathetic creature to the *yunka* man, holding it up to him like an offering to the gods.

"By my feet!" the man commanded, and my heart soared to watch Ucho humiliated like this in front of so many people. I was sure he would take out his anger on me later, but even so, it was a good moment.

At the single word "Go!" Ucho ran off, far away from the watchful eyes of the people. Then the stranger turned his attention to me again, and I was not so glad of this. What did he want with me? I squirmed and tried to escape again, but his hand only held my shoulder more tightly. I scanned the crowd. Chasca and Mama clutched each other as they moved closer to me, but most of the people stood still, curious to see what this stranger would do next. Would they allow this man to harm me, even if I was the Ugly One? I didn't think so.

The *yunka* stranger lifted his free hand toward my face. Immediately, I slapped my own hand over the scar—an added layer of protection on top of the hair that already covered the cheek. It was foolish of me to do so. Everyone knew the scar was there. Nothing I had tried could make it disappear.

The stranger's hand hovered in the air, as if ready to strike me. He leaned his face closer to mine and narrowed his eyes. They were such a dark brown that it was difficult to tell where the color ended and the center blackness began. He probed me with these eyes, searching my thoughts, my spirit. I felt as if my very heart was being observed by this stranger, and somehow his stare slowed the beating. It was an odd sensation, having someone control my heartbeat with his eyes. I wondered how he did it and if he would make my heart stop altogether. And then I ceased wondering anything, and all I saw were his huge dark eyes.

His fingers moved to the river scar on my cheek, and I was surprised to find that my hand was no longer covering it. Gently, he lifted my hair shield, revealing the ugly scar for everyone to see. Why I didn't stop this I cannot say, but I know it had something to do with the way his eyes had not left mine. It was impossible to look away, to move.

He traced the scar lightly with his index finger, starting at the top by the eyebrow. No person had ever touched my scar before. This was the part of myself that I kept the most hidden, and it felt as if he were touching the inside of my head, setting it on fire. Still I didn't move, and his finger finished its journey to the corner of my lip and rested there for a moment. His eyes held mine steadily, and he uttered one word: *"Ari."* Yes. Gently, he removed his hand and looked down at the animal at his feet.

Freed from his gaze, my thoughts came together and became my own again. I noticed that the people were watching us, and this was when I realized my cheek was still exposed. Quickly, I covered it with my hair.

The *yunka* man lifted the animal and held it in front

of me, and again he said, *"Ari."* I took it from him, unsure if this was what he wanted me to do. It fit into my palm, and I saw that it was a jungle bird, a baby macaw. One last time he said *"Ari,"* and then he walked back to his trading goods.

The crowd was slow to break up, but a few people followed the man to continue trading. Others stood and watched me, curious to see what I would do. The tiny bird didn't stir, except perhaps for a small rise and fall of its chest. Or maybe it was just my hand shaking? I wondered what I should do with it.

Chasca and Mama rushed to me, and my sister touched my arm. "Micay?" she asked, her eyes full of concern.

"Just leave me be," I said. I pulled free, too humiliated to say more. Not far away was my basket, overturned in the dirt, a reminder of Ucho and his cruel words. I scrambled to pick up the scattered wool that hadn't blown away and placed it back inside the basket. Carefully, I rested the bird on the soft wool. Then, without looking at the crowd or my family, hoping that no one would follow me, I ran away, back to my rock.

2
SUMAC
HUANACAURI
Handsome Rainbow

MY rock wasn't just a rock. It was a *huaca,* a special stone that contained spirit powers. I told no one of this. If the people knew, they would also come. It was my alone place, not for them. As I sat on my rock, the spirit within calmed me, told me all was well. No one had followed me. The stranger wasn't here. I was safe. *Ari.*

The little bird was resting in the basket, cushioned by the pile of white wool, and I saw that it was, indeed, breathing — tiny, fast breaths that moved the wool up and down. But I had to look closely to see this.

Sumac Huanacauri was a sorry-looking thing, mostly bald, with clumps of dirty reddish feathers sticking out of its body. At once I felt a connection to it, for it, also, was ugly. I wanted it to open its eyes and see me, to know me. But it was not well, this tiny one, and so it kept its bluish lids closed and breathed its fast little breaths.

Water. It should have water and food as well, I realized. But there was no water up at the *huaca*, and I didn't want to leave just yet. I did have a pouch of dried potatoes that I kept stored by the rock, because sometimes I didn't feel like leaving to eat with the others. I pulled one out and held the shriveled pale potato up to the bird's beak.

It did nothing.

I thought of the mother *caracara* bird who made her nest on the large rock behind the *molle* tree just last spring. She fed her children from her beak. Feeling foolish, I placed the potato between my lips and put my face close to its beak. It opened its eyes a crack but made no motion to eat. Then it closed its eyes again.

The potato was beginning to grow moist and sag. I took it into my mouth and chewed, enjoying the flavor. The bird slit its eyes to watch and craned its neck, stretching it long and thin. In quick, light motions, it nibbled at my lips with its dirty beak. I pushed a piece of half-chewed potato mush out of my mouth, and it took this into its own and swallowed eagerly.

Ahh. I understood now. The food needed to be wet, easy to chew. I took another piece of potato and mashed it between my teeth. When it was good and soft, I rested a clump on my tongue and stuck this out for the hungry bird. Immediately, it began to scrape the surface, eagerly picking up bits of food, which slid down its throat in fast little bumps.

I smiled. "You are hungry, little one?" I asked in a quiet voice. The small bird stuck its neck out for more, and I fed it in this manner two more dried pieces, until it didn't lift its head any longer. Its eyes closed and its head lowered in sleep, the breathing easier, a bit slower now. Good. Already I knew that I wanted this creature to live, to be with me. I didn't know how the *yunka* stranger was able to see so much about me so quickly, for I believed I hid my secret feelings well, but somehow the man knew that I needed this bird, and this was something that I hadn't even known about myself.

I watched it resting in the basket, comfortable even though I was so close. It was the kind of bird that grew the beautiful long red feathers Uncle Turu was trading for earlier. But it was still very young and very ugly. It was hard to imagine that it could ever look anything *but* ugly. The *yunka* man had called it Sumac Huanacauri. Handsome Rainbow. This was a very big and hopeful name for such a sad little creature. I wondered if such a name could offend the gods. Perhaps for now it would just be Sumac. Even this seemed ridiculous. Calling this scrawny bird Handsome One? But then Muti's call from earlier — *Look, the Ugly One is here. Millay shows her face!* — echoed in my mind, and anger swelled in my belly.

"Sumac," I said aloud, daring the rocks to question the name. "You are Sumac." The bird looked up at me, and I placed my hand on his head and stroked it lightly. He tilted it to the side, as if in thought. "What are you thinking, Sumac?" I asked. But whatever he might have said he held within.

Sumac remained silent all afternoon as I cleaned the remaining alpaca fur for Mama. He slept and slept, healing himself from a long journey that was beyond any travels I had ever known.

My thoughts wandered as my fingers worked their way through the fleece with a knowledge that came from having done this task for many years. Ucho's words still echoed in my ears. I wanted to leave them behind, to forget, to not be bothered by his taunts, but we are not always able to do what we want. In my memory, the stick poked into my side over and over again, and I grew angry once more. Why did I have to be the Ugly One? Why couldn't I have smooth skin like every other girl in the village? Why wouldn't the gods remove my scar and heal me? It made no sense that I should suffer this way.

I put down the fleece and grabbed a handful of mud from the earth. Angrily, I brought it to my face, rubbing it along my cheeks and forehead to cover the skin and offensive scar. I had learned that mud dried quickly in Inti's hot rays and, if put on properly, gave the temporary feeling of a smooth face. The challenge was not to cry, for tears would run down my cheeks in tiny rivers, preventing the mud from drying well and giving it a bumpy texture. More than once I had ruined a mask in this manner.

I turned my face to Inti so he could kiss it with his warm, drying rays.

"Is it done yet?" my sister's voice asked from behind.

I jumped. She had startled me that much.

"I didn't know you were here!" I said in an accusing voice. "When did you begin sneaking up on people?" I was embarrassed. No one had ever witnessed my mud ritual, and I prided myself on being aware of my surroundings so that I wasn't taken by surprise as I just had been.

"I don't sneak up on people. I sneak up on *you*," she said with a laugh as she sat down by my side.

"Why are you here, Chasca?"

"I came to tell you Mama needs our help preparing dinner. Uncle Turu is telling stories tonight, and we don't want to be late." Here she paused and offered a sly smile. "But you seemed so busy, I didn't want to interrupt you, Mudface."

"Mudface, you say?" I replied with my own smile. I stuck my finger into the earth and, before she could stop me, smeared a streak across Chasca's cheek.

I thought my older sister might be mad at me, but her expression was one of concern, not anger. "Micay, why do you cover your face in mud?" she asked quietly.

I didn't like this question. The answer seemed obvious enough. Why force me to speak of it? "It feels pleasant on my skin," I lied. I didn't like being dishonest, especially with Chasca, but I disliked talking about my scar even more.

"Micay," she said in a serious tone, "I wish you wouldn't hide your face. Ucho and those boys are very young and very foolish."

I gazed at the ground. "I don't know what you mean."

She continued as though I hadn't spoken. "They don't see what a special person you truly are. If they did, they would never taunt you as they do."

Hot tears trickled down my face. Somehow the ones on the right side always found the scar beneath the mud quickly. I could feel them course their way down my cheek, exposing the ugly, ruined skin.

Chasca finally let the topic be. "Mama is waiting for us. We should go," she said. Then, with one last attempt at humor, she added, "But we should wash first, Mud-face."

I smiled at her, and a salty drop of tear and mud caught on the edge of my lip. "Yes, and we should hurry," I said. "I don't want to be late for Uncle Turu's storytelling. That is my favorite time."

"I know," Chasca said. "You always say that."

I took the basket with the still-sleeping bird in one hand and my sister's palm in the other. Together, we made our way to the stream, then down the mountain, so we wouldn't be late for dinner and Uncle Turu's storytelling.

3
MANCO CAPAC
AND MAMA OCLLO
Son of the Sun
and Daughter of the Moon

Ñ̃AWPA *pachapi,* once upon a time, there was only darkness. Then Inti, the great Sun Lord, took pity on the wretched creatures of the earth and sent his son, Manco Capac, to spread civilization." Uncle Turu took a step closer to the fire and paused, for he enjoyed the silences of a good telling as much as the words. He searched the faces of his listeners, the people of the village, to make sure no one interrupted the quiet. Ucho and the other boys sat at the edge of the crowd, pointing and whispering at the *yunka* stranger, who was watching Uncle Turu intently. As Uncle Turu's eyes reached the boys, they stopped whispering and let their hands fall to the ground.

This was one of my favorite tales, the story of our people. I leaned in closer, not wanting to miss any of it. But I was still careful to stay far enough from the fire that the light couldn't reach my face. I pulled the edges of my woolen cloak close under my chin to keep away the outside chill and hugged Sumac to my chest. Listen now, and you can judge for yourself how skilled my uncle was in the storytelling ways.

"The Moon Goddess sent her daughter, Mama Ocllo, to be Manco Capac's bride," Uncle Turu said. "Then Mama Ocllo and Manco Capac set out on their journey to bring civilization and enlightenment to the earth. Rainbow God created a beautiful bridge for them, connecting the world of the sky to the world of the land. The husband and wife held hands and walked down it to the earth below."

Uncle Turu lifted his hands and made an arc to show the rainbow bridge. Then he linked them as Manco Capac and Mama Ocllo did so long ago. The fire flickered and threw strange shadow patterns on his hands, making them seem bigger, then smaller.

"The bridge ended at Lake Titicaca. The waters were lovely and deep. The couple washed and smiled, enjoying this new feeling of water on their bodies. But they didn't stay there long, for they had much to do. Inti had made a golden staff of his own body and given it to his son. He told Manco Capac to travel throughout the land in search of the center of the world, for this would be the place where he should begin a city. 'You will know when you have found this place, because the golden staff will sink deep into the earth and disappear,' he said."

Uncle Turu spread his hands, palms down, and moved them out and away from his body, into the distance. "They traveled for a long time, always heading in the direction the staff pointed. And finally they came to a place that Mama Ocllo and Manco Capac felt to be right and true. Manco Capac lifted the brilliant staff above his head" — Uncle Turu lifted his own hands high above his head as if he were holding a long stick — "and thrust it into the earth." He lowered his hands in a quick gesture. "The stick glowed more brightly and beautifully as it touched the ground, so that Manco Capac and Mama Ocllo had to shield their faces. Then it sank below the surface, out of sight.

"The husband and wife knew that they had found Cuzco, the center of the world. Manco Capac taught the men how to farm the land, and Mama Ocllo showed the women how to weave. Civilization came to the people, and Cuzco was the center of it all, a thriving city of nobles and priests. All the children of Manco Capac and Mama Ocllo grew strong and wise and had their own children. We are the descendants of these people. And this means that each one of us is born of the mighty sun Inti, the father of us all. So it was and ever shall be."

The people solemnly repeated, "So it was and ever shall be." Then there was silence. I closed my eyes and listened to the crackling of the fire. Its warmth didn't reach me strongly, but I imagined it was day and that Inti was still with us, touching me with his long golden fingers.

The *yunka* man was nodding his head in agreement. He pointed to himself and said, "*Ari*. Why I go to Sacred Sun City."

I thought I had misunderstood. Many people traveled to Cuzco, the grand city where the Sapa Inca, our emperor, lived. But I had never heard of one who would go to Sacred Sun City, a place hidden high in the mountains. Did the stranger mean he was traveling there?

Sacred Sun City, the Sapa Inca's most precious estate. My heart raced at the thought of this religious center where only the holiest of priests and the most beautiful of Sun Maidens lived, always in prayer and praise to Inti and the other gods. How could he, a *yunka* stranger, feel that he was worthy to go there? He wasn't even one of Inti's true children. He would be killed — thrown into a pit of poisonous snakes or fed to hungry jaguars — before he would be allowed to enter such a sacred place. Surely I had misunderstood.

It wasn't my place to ask, but Yawar, the leader of our village, spoke out. "You are making the journey to Sacred Sun City at Machu Picchu?" His eyebrows were raised high in question, and his voice didn't hide his surprise.

"*Ari*. Sacred Sun City. Praise Inti."

"They will kill you before you can pass through the Sun Gate and enter the city," Yawar said. This wasn't a question. He spoke in a flat voice, stating the fact that it was.

The stranger showed no sign that he was frightened by these words. "No. Not kill. I go. Praise Inti. Touch Sacred Rock. Ask question."

The Sacred Rock was a *huaca* in Sacred Sun City. It was said to have the strongest of spirit powers. If you asked it a question in the proper manner, and if you were worthy, it would answer. It could solve your troubles, make them disappear, like a scar on a cheek suddenly vanishing forever. But very few were allowed contact with the Sacred Rock.

"What do you want to ask it?" Muti blurted out.

"No. Only here." The stranger pointed to his chest. He may have been journeying to his death, but he was at least wise enough to keep his question guarded within himself.

Yawar stood tall in front of the dancing, hissing fire.

He walked to the stranger and placed a large hand on his shoulder. "You must be permitted to enter by the Sapa Inca himself, and not many are worthy of speaking to the Sacred Rock. You are from far away, so perhaps you do not know these things. It would be best if you didn't go."

"I am holiest. I am worthy," the stranger said loudly. He had been looking at Yawar, but now he turned his head in my direction, and I felt little bumps crawl on the back of my neck. It was as if he could see through the night air, directly to my hidden face. "We know who we are," he added. Then he made a fist and pounded his chest, his face fierce. "Here."

No one said a word. No one moved. The jungle stranger was still staring at me, although he couldn't possibly see me hidden in the darkness. I tucked my knees in under my chin and tightened the cloak around my face, afraid that he would pull me out of the crowd. But no. Instead he rose and walked stiffly away from the gathered people. Alone in the dark, his figure was quickly lost to my sight, as if he had disappeared from the earth forever.

4
MUSQUKUTI
Dreamtime

IN our *wasi,* our one-room house, later that night, my family prepared for bedtime. The *wasi* was sturdy, built of tightly stacked stones with a thick thatched roof, but it could not protect us from the creeping fingers of the cold night air. We piled blankets and weavings over our bodies by the light of the hearth, which still glowed faintly from the evening meal preparations. I'd fed Sumac again, and he was nestled into the center of a basket filled with warm alpaca wool, just to the side of my rush mat. Now I lay back and pulled up my favorite wool blanket, a beautiful red one with weavings of the sun and birds.

As I turned to my right side, the position I always slept in to hide my scar, Mama knelt next to me. With a small smile, she tucked the blanket under my chin. Her hand lingered, and she tentatively brushed the hair off my smooth cheek. She was my mother, so she had to do this, but I believed she didn't truly want to touch me. When she leaned in to kiss me, I turned away as I always did, so her lips were spared the pain of touching my ugly face.

With a sad sigh, Mama stood. I wasn't certain if her sorrow came from gazing on her daughter's scarred face or from being a mother who longed to kiss her child but was rejected night after night. It was probably a mix of both. I turned away because it was easier not to discover the truth. I know this sounds odd. Why not let my mother kiss me? But what if she did, and it was so horrible for her that she never wanted to do so again? This was as close as I came to my beautiful Mama every day, and I cherished the moment despite her sadness. By turning away, I ensured that she would try again the next night. I told myself this was almost the same as a good-night kiss.

"Did I not say a stranger would come?" Papa asked from under his blanket, satisfaction thick in his voice.

"Yes, my husband," Mama responded quietly. I saw her kiss Chasca before joining Papa. My older brother, Hatun, had been gone for almost three years now, serving his time repairing and guarding roads for the emperor as all young men did, but every night I thought of him at this moment. Mama would have kissed him good night after Chasca.

"No, you did *not* say a stranger would come," Chasca said as she slid under her covers next to me. The reflection from the hearth danced in her bright brown eyes. From the way the corners of her eyes crinkled, I knew that she was smiling. She found Papa very funny and liked to goad him. In her playful voice she added, "You complained that your foot hurt, Papa. You never said a stranger was coming."

"Is that not the same?" Papa defended himself. "It is said that a pained foot is a sure sign a stranger will visit."

"Perhaps," Chasca said. "If you didn't complain of aches and pains most days."

"I am an old man. Show the respect due an elder," Papa snapped.

"Yes, Papa," Chasca said obediently, but I could hear the smile in her voice.

"I was certain of his arrival. And I am certain the man is a fool," Papa went on. "He should go back to the *yunka*."

Mama, who often kept Papa calm with her soothing

voice, murmured from under the covers, "That would seem wise."

"What good does it do him, stomping through the mountains only to be killed? He is a fool!" Papa's voice rose in pitch as it grew louder.

"Ahh," Chasca said, "but sometimes even fools are correct, Papa. Perhaps they won't kill him."

"Ridiculous!" Papa's voice howled like the wind as he continued. "He isn't even a child of Inti! Chasca, don't say such stupid things, or the bat will pay you a visit." Papa made this threat at least once a day, that the bat would come and visit one of us. It was said that if a bat entered your home, you would meet with great misfortune. Papa was always worrying that some disaster would befall our family.

Chasca didn't share his worry. She sat up slightly and sighed. "I fear he may already have done so, Papa. I may have seen the fluttering of wings as I awoke this morning." She paused and scratched her head, then added, "Or perhaps not. It was still dark, and I had sleep in my eyes."

"Chasca!" Mama hissed. "Do not tempt the gods." Mama didn't worry about bats in houses the way Papa did, but she didn't like to hear Chasca say such things. And my sister often said things to bother Papa. She was very pretty, Chasca, but at times she didn't know when to be silent.

"But I really might have, Mama. It flew out the doorway before I could be sure," she said.

Suddenly, Papa sat up and shouted, "Ha!" The sound startled Sumac, whose little head jutted up above the edge of the basket at my side. I reached over and stroked him lightly.

Mama, who was used to Papa's loud noises, said calmly, "What is it, husband?"

"It is a bad omen if the bat visits you at twilight," Papa said. "Chasca may have seen one *as she awoke*. It was morning, not twilight. There is no danger."

I could hear in his voice that he was pleased with himself, like a child who has just answered an old man's riddle correctly.

With this settled, the small *wasi* filled with the gentle noises of the night. The little group of *quwis* Mama was raising scuttled about in the corners, making their quiet squeaking calls. The wind danced with the tree outside our home, and the leaves made their soft flutter music.

I closed my eyes and watched the blackness under my eyelids. But it didn't stay dark for long. The image of the *yunka* stranger appeared before me. His face was fierce. I didn't want to think of this man. I opened my eyes and stared at the ceiling. It bothered me, this image of the jungle man. Something hadn't been said that should have been. I was unsure if anyone else was awake, but I whispered my words anyway. "Perhaps he really is chosen by Inti."

No one responded. I didn't know if they were all asleep or if they didn't hear me or if they didn't want to talk of the stranger any longer. I closed my eyes and turned to my right side, the position I always slept in to hide my scar. I hoped that the stranger would stay out of my dreams this night.

If you have ever heard a story told well, then you know what happened next. Of course I dreamt of the *yunka* stranger. They say that the dream world is closest to the spirit world, that to know your dreams is to know the past, the present, and the future. That night I walked with the spirits as I dreamt.

At first I sat on my *huaca,* my special rock. The stars in the great star river hung bright and heavy and seemed very close. The surrounding mountains were huge, dark living things that reached up, up, up, and touched the tiny, bright flecks of light that lived in the night sky.

The *huaca* grew hot, as if from Inti, but it wasn't

his time in the sky. It was a good feeling, this warmth, and it made the rock soft like the coat of a baby llama. I slowly sank, as if in thick water, but this didn't frighten me. I was pleased that I would finally meet the spirit that lived within.

Inside was a dark cave. A black jaguar with gleaming eyes paced in the corner. She growled a warning: "Not yet." Then her back muscles bunched together, and she took a mighty leap out of the cave.

Suddenly, the *yunka* stranger stood before me. His eyes held me once more so that my feet were stuck to the ground and I could only wave my arms like branches swaying lightly in the breeze. He stepped back and held something out for me, but I couldn't see what it was. Staring at me, he squatted and placed this object onto the ground. Then he stood tall and spread his arms. Something pushed through his skin and grew like many pieces of thin red grass. His body shrank and was covered in this redness, but some was also blue and yellow. He flapped his arms and — oh — it was *feathers* that he had grown. He was a bird, regal and beautiful. With a great macaw call of *BRRRUAW,* he sprang up and flapped off into the distance, so that I could no longer see him.

And it was then that I was able to move my feet again. I stepped forward and looked to the ground to see what it was that he wanted me to have. A lone toadstool stuck out of the earth. It was small with a creamy brown head. Carefully, I lifted it from the soil. It was soft and delicate like the petals of the lily flower. I placed this toadstool inside my basket, making sure that it was cradled by the alpaca wool. I hugged the basket close to me like a mother protecting her newborn child.

When I emerged from the cave and was back on top of the *huaca*, it was Sumac who sat in the basket, resting comfortably in the white fleece, staring up at me with big dark eyes. I was glad to see the little bird, but I couldn't remember what it was that I had first put into the basket. I knew it was important, a message of some sort, a gift from the jungle stranger. But it was gone, the memory slipping away like a leaf floating down the river.

◙◙

I was always the first of my family to awaken. I didn't like to think that someone might arise and see me still in sleep, perhaps with my cheek exposed. So I was surprised when I opened my eyes to Chasca, who was staring over me with a scowl on her face. I realized at once I was lying on my back. My face wasn't covered. She was scowling because she saw my hideous scar.

But no, my mind cleared a bit, and I heard Sumac

making little raspy *eeeee* sounds in the basket to my right. They weren't loud, but Chasca was a light sleeper, and immediately I understood why her face was un-happy.

"Make it stop," she grumbled, and rolled back onto her mat, mumbling as she settled into sleep again. She had never been entirely awake.

The rolling chirp of the crickets passed through the early-morning air. From the warmth of my blankets I could see that it was almost time for Inti to rise. Light pinks and purples, the color of the *munca* flowers, were beginning to creep through the mountains.

Sumac hadn't stopped. Little *eeeee eeeee*s were scratching their way out of his throat. I threw off my woolen bed coverings, and the cold morning air splashed my body. Tiny bumps rose along my arms and legs. I could feel each of the hairs standing tall and straight, like feathers growing out of my skin. Memories flooded me. The *yunka* man had been in my dream! Suddenly, I knew I must find him. He had an important message. Sumac looked up at me with his dark bird eyes and stopped his noises. Grabbing his basket and my cloak, I rushed outside.

The clouds were thick in the air, weaving in and out among the soaring heights of the mountaintops. Mama Killa, the moon, rested in the sky, round and heavy, but she was leaving even as I watched. The still-frozen gray-green *ichu* grass made a *crunch crunch* sound as I walked hurriedly toward the center of our small village.

I spotted him easily — a figure walking along the mountain trail high in the distance. At first I thought to chase after this man, the *yunka* stranger. But he was very far away, so far that he appeared smaller than Sumac hunched in his little basket.

I watched the *yunka* man, his back to me, as he climbed higher on the path. And then it was as if he felt my eyes upon him, for he stopped and turned and looked in my direction. The clouds hung just above his head and sent down small tendrils that caressed him. *Why have you stopped?* they seemed to ask. He ignored the questioning clouds and continued to face me, and I felt a strong pull from him and from the city to which he was headed. But I couldn't follow. This was his journey. I was meant to stay.

Sumac let out a screech. He was shivering in his basket, his few feathers ruffled in a sad attempt to keep warm. I glanced once more at the distant mountain, but the stranger was gone, as I knew he would be. Only the clouds remained, beckoning to me with their long, moving fingers. *Come this way, child,* they gestured. The breeze blew against my face, cold and busy. *Follow him,* it whispered as it streamed by.

But these were foolish thoughts. I was only a girl, a very ugly girl. When Sumac squawked for attention again, I was relieved to turn away and head back to the warmth of the *wasi*. Still, as my feet crunched the *ichu* grass, my mind went back to the twisting trail and the man who followed it to fulfill his right and true path. He had frightened me, this *yunka* stranger who made my heart slow and revealed my scar to the people. But odd as it may seem, I hoped I would see him again.

5
PAQO
Shaman

I pulled my wrap more tightly about my shoulders as I hurried toward the warmth of my family's *wasi*. Sumac trembled in his basket. I leaned in and blew warm breath on his tiny body.

The sound of someone playing the *antara*, wooden pipes, alone and quiet, suddenly filled the early morning. I paused. The faint music slipped and slithered through the air, insisting that I follow it. Where did it come from?

It is a strange thing, the way your feet can turn and lead you in a different direction than expected. *Go to the* wasi *to sit by the hearth. Turn back,* my thoughts whispered, but my feet were more certain, and I followed the call of the music. The grass crunched quietly, as if even the earth was frightened of where I was headed.

The *antara* led me to the home of the great Paqo, the

powerful shaman of our people. His *wasi* sat alone on the edge of the mountain, away from the other homes. The Paqo had moved to our village several years earlier. It was said that he had once been a great priest in the capital city of Cuzco, that he had worked for the mighty Sapa Inca himself. No one really knew why he had left such a position of honor, although there were many wagging tongues and interesting stories that tried to explain his mysterious appearance in our small village. I had been a young child and didn't remember his arrival. To me, he had always been there on the edge of village life, like a watchful jaguar to be tiptoed around carefully.

The music beckoned from within the Paqo's *wasi*. Why it had brought me here I didn't understand. I paused at the entrance, setting my hair carefully over my cheek. Surely I wasn't meant to enter. One so powerful as the great Paqo would be most offended by such a loathsome face as mine. His time was spent with the gods, not with the people. I shouldn't be here. I had no right. And yet, this was a place of spirit and magic. The Paqo dwelled with the gods. He and Inti were as one. I had always felt this power when the Paqo was near, but my fear of him had kept me away.

A red and brown alpaca cloth hung in the doorway. It was adorned with a pattern of woven hummingbirds that flitted about playfully. Sumac let out a low squawk. *Go in,* he seemed to say. I ran my fingers through my hair once more, to be certain the offensive scar was well hidden, but still I stood, uncertain.

Suddenly, the *antara* stopped speaking. The silence of the early-morning chill settled upon me. A voice from inside, low and even, said, "The bird is cold. Come in."

I remained as unmoving as the mountains, still unsure what to do.

The voice spoke more forcefully. "Come in!"

Finally, I pushed the weaving aside and stepped into the *wasi.* On the floor sat the great Paqo, his eyes closed, a peaceful smile upon his lips. A small *antara* of six bound wooden pipes rested by his side. The *wasi* was dim. Still, a faint light from the hearth glimmered on the gold plugs hanging from his ears, a sign of his high status. How he was aware that I had been standing outside I didn't know.

His eyes remained closed.

I let the weaving fall back into place behind me.

"I have been waiting for you," he said. "An entire life can slip away downstream in hiding."

What did he mean? The air was warm and heavy with the scent of burnt *koka* leaves, a smell I recognized from ceremonies of the past. Odd dried plants and flowers hung from the ceiling, and the walls were covered with pictures of Inti and Mama Killa, as well as of the stars, the rainbow, and Illapa, the thunder god. A painted river snaked its way along one wall, and carved condors soared toward the roof. Behind the Paqo, a large weaving of a jaguar stared at me with yellow eyes. Its teeth gleamed, as if it were ready to eat me for its next meal.

"Sit!" The Paqo's eyes opened abruptly. They were like the eyes of the *yunka* stranger, not to be ignored.

I sat.

"The scar distracts you from Beyond."

His words were a riddle. I grasped my hair, holding it tightly against my cheek to guard against the shaman's eyes.

"The past is the key to the now," he went on, and the jaguar hanging behind him hissed. Or perhaps it was the embers crackling and spitting on the hearth. "Tell me, what do you remember of your past?"

What *did* I remember of my past? Sitting on my *huaca*. Hiding my face from the people. Searching for a way to make my scar leave me forever. Lurking at the far edge of the fire, always away from the people and the eyes and the words that stung.

"There isn't much to remember," I replied.

"Oh?" His eyes probed, as if they would force me

to speak my secrets, much as the *yunka* stranger had made me reveal my face.

"Why am I here?" I asked. It was fear of what I might say that gave me the courage to ask a question of so powerful a person.

"Yes. Why are you here?" he asked, and his lips opened in a smile that showed he was missing his top two front teeth.

His question startled me. "I shouldn't be. I'm sorry to intrude."

"Does the river apologize when it changes its path after the rains?" he asked.

To answer incorrectly would be shameful; to say nothing, disrespectful. My head whirled from the strong scent of the *koka* and the confusing way the shaman mixed his words. "I don't know."

"Of course it doesn't. It follows its nature, as you must do. But you were right."

I was right? Choosing correct words in this place of confusion seemed impossible.

He closed his eyes and picked up the *antara*. His nails, I noticed, were yellowed and very long, like the claws of a beast. There was a frightening quiet before he said, "You should not be here."

I had done a terrible thing, coming to this man's home. Who would dare to interrupt the mighty shaman but an ugly, scorned girl? The scar had ruined more than the skin on my face. It had twisted me inside.

"You should not be here because you aren't ready," the Paqo said. "Come back when the bird says so."

He held the *antara* to his lips and began to play. The music was slow and deep and sad. It said that I must leave.

"I'm sorry to have disturbed you," I whispered. He didn't reply, but continued playing. Cradling Sumac's basket under my arm, I stood. My head spun for a moment, and the music hopped and swirled. Then I pushed the door weaving out of my way, stumbling out of the *wasi* before the *antara* could turn hurtful in its song.

The cool air cleared my thoughts. Inti shone brightly above. I had missed the morning greeting to the sun. Did he understand why? Was he angry with me? I couldn't bear the thought. Inti was the only companion I had.

Sumac squawked insistently. He opened his beak toward my face, and his small gray tongue probed the air. He was hungry. I didn't know what the Paqo meant, that the bird would tell me when to return. I was simply glad to be leaving, and I knew I would never come back.

As I quickened my step, the music stopped. I paused

on the path, my ears straining to catch the tune. Instead, a new sound wound its way to me: the Paqo laughing heartily from within his *wasi*. I turned and fled, his laughter chasing after me like the wind.

6
PACHAMAMA
Earth Mother

Ayau hailli, ayau hailli!
Kapai Inti, Apu Yaya,
Kaway kuri, sumay kuri.
Song of praise and victory!
Great Sun, mighty father,
Wake the seeds and make them grow.

The men sang as they lifted their *tacclas*, their foot plows, straight above their heads. Their skin glowed with sweat in the early-morning sun as they hurled their tools downward and jumped on them with their feet to grind them into the soft earth.

Hailli, Pachamama, hailli!
Victory, oh, Earth Mother, victory!

The girls and women answered back as they scattered the corn seeds into the turned soil. It was sowing season, a time of great joy and solemn sacrifice and prayer. Boys stood by with their slings, ready to scare away any birds or small animals that might try to make an easy meal of our hard work.

There had been many preparations for this day. In all of the *wasis,* the people presented offerings of maize-flour dough, shells, colorful stones, plucked eyelashes, and freshly killed rabbits. Papa had wrapped a beautiful cob of corn, the bright color of Inti's rays, in our family's finest cloth and placed it in a niche in the wall, chanting over and over to Inti and to Pachamama, Earth Mother, to make this harvest plentiful. Rain had been scarce for several years now, and the storehouses were not so well stocked as they used to be. If Earth Mother remained dry and empty, if she didn't give us a beautiful golden crop this year, the people would go hungry. Papa was even more fearful than usual of bad omens. Every hoot of an owl sent him into a high-pitched fit, and whenever the cooking fire hissed, he threw a bit of *aca,* maize beer, into the flames to appease their anger.

Only the great Paqo could be sure of the proper day to begin planting. He knew the language of the stars, and he spoke with them every night, waiting until they told him the time was right and true. When he announced to the people that it would be today, the final preparations were made. We arose before dawn and danced our way out to the fields. The first ground was broken by our leader, Yawar, just as Inti began to rise in the sky.

I had felt concern that Sumac might try to eat the seeds as I planted them, but he sat on my right shoulder, studying all around him with curiosity. He was strong enough to perch there now and was beginning to show signs that he would live up to his name, Handsome One. Small feathers, rich red and deep blue, were appearing, and he was growing larger on the many potatoes and corn kernels I fed him. But he was still young and couldn't fly. He had chosen my right shoulder as his favorite perch, as if he knew it would free me of my worry to keep my right cheek covered by my hair.

"Why do you bother to plant the seeds?" a voice sneered from behind. Without turning, I knew who it was. Ucho. He continued speaking, even though I didn't acknowledge his words. "Surely Earth Mother is offended that the Ugly One would place seeds into her. They won't grow! Don't waste our precious kernels by contaminating them with your hand!"

This wasn't the first time I had heard such words. When I was younger, I had made it a point to study the location of the maize and potatoes I had planted and had snuck back to the fields to see if they had grown. I didn't want to offend Pachamama, and if she felt I wasn't worthy to plant, then I would not have done so again. But my corn grew tall and golden, my potatoes were abundant. It was a great relief to learn I wasn't completely scorned by the gods.

"I know that you hear me," Ucho said menacingly. "And now you have brought a pest that will eat our sacred crops!"

Suddenly, I heard a light whizzing sound by my ear, and Sumac screeched so loudly, it echoed within my head. It took me a moment to realize that Ucho had used his sling to throw a stone at Sumac. It hit the bird's right wing, which Sumac lifted high in the air as he squawked in pain. I brought him to my chest to protect and comfort him. There was no blood, but my anger was fierce.

Ucho stood laughing, unaware that behind him the Paqo had appeared as if by magic, tall and severe. The Paqo stood silently, listening to Ucho's laughter, observing my reaction, watching me with his dark eyes. When I did nothing, he raised his hands and spoke to the people. "It is time to meet at the field guardian rock," he announced.

Abruptly, Ucho stopped laughing. He was clearly

startled by the Paqo's sudden presence behind him, but he gave me a final sneer before he moved toward the rock with the people. The Paqo studied my face a moment more before he, too, turned and made his way to the center of the fields.

I hope you don't judge me too harshly for saying nothing. I was frightened of Ucho, and to fear someone is to give him power over you, the power to silence your voice and cause you to hide your face from the world.

Ucho was cruel, and I was a coward, and the Paqo had witnessed it all and said nothing. Still cradling Sumac, I dropped to the ground. With my free hand I grabbed a fistful of dirt in frustration. I wanted to dig a hole in Pachamama and scream all of my rage and humiliation into her body. I would scream so loudly and for so long that I would yell away all the years of hurt built up inside me. I wanted Pachamama to take it all from me, and then I would fill in this screaming hole and be done with it. But how could I do this to Earth Mother, especially during planting season? How could I place all that anger and grief inside her body? Nothing would grow. What tiny seed could survive such pain?

I stood and wiped my hands on my wrap. Slowly, I made my way to the guardian rock and the gathered people. I held the Handsome One closely and whispered to him as I petted his head, asking him to forgive me for my weakness, for allowing him to be injured. The bird remained still against my chest, except for occasionally letting out a squawk and stretching out his right wing as though to see if it was still sore.

The guardian rock sat tall and proud in the midst of our fields. It was a living rock, for it had not been placed there by the people's hands. Taller than Uncle Turu by a head, it had protected and fertilized our crops and received our prayers and sacrifices from the time of our ancestors.

As the people approached the guardian, each placed a small stone collected from the fields onto a pile at its foot. Many kissed their fingers and backed away reverently.

The great Paqo came last. For the ceremony, he wore richly colored garments and a headdress with two golden-yellow feathers. His body clinked and clanked with each step, for he had attached golden bells to his knees and ankles. A brown pouch hung from his shoulder. The people cleared a path for him, and he walked directly to the rock and bowed low at the waist. With a flourish, he stood tall, kissed his fingertips gently, and raised his arms high above his head. Then he took out a small golden bowl filled with dried *koka* leaves and set it in front of the rock.

As we watched, he ripped off the tips of his long fingernails one after another and placed them within the bowl, on top of the *koka*. Carefully, he set fire to the mixture. The leaves twisted and writhed in the flames, and a pungent smell tickled my nose before the smoke was lost to the sky. The people stood in silence as the offering burned itself out. With one mighty breath, the Paqo blew the ashes directly up and onto the proud guardian rock.

Yawar led a llama, pure white and unblemished, to the front of the people. Then, in a booming voice, the great Paqo spoke directly to Inti: "May you always remain as young as you were on the first day, giving light and warmth forever!" To the rock he prayed, "You who have watered our land for so many years, through which blessing we gather our food, do the same this year also, and give even more water for a harvest greater yet!"

Many people joined in this prayer now, shouting "*Hailli!* Victory!"

In one fluid motion, the mighty Paqo pulled his *tumi*, his ceremonial knife, from his shoulder pouch. As Yawar held the chosen llama steady, the Paqo plunged the knife deep into its chest. The animal cried out — kicking its legs frantically as the people shouted, *Hailli! Hailli!* — then died swiftly, its death in honor of mighty Inti and sacred Pachamama. The Paqo filled the golden bowl with the llama's blood and placed it at the foot of the guardian rock. I thought I detected a quick scowl on the shaman's face, but then it was gone. Many spirits, some kind and some mischievous, hovered near us at such a sacred time, and one of them may have tried a trick of some sort. It wouldn't make sense for the Paqo to be scowling while honoring the gods so well.

Several boys took out their wooden *quena quena* flutes and began to play. To the sound of our singing, we made our way from the fields to prepare and enjoy a village feast. We had fasted for several days in preparation for the sowing, and there is nothing to bring joy to your step so much as the thought of a savory meal after a long day spent in the fields.

7
YURAQ SARA
White Corn

UNCLE Turu stood before the fire. There were smiles on many faces, for we had feasted well on deer and *quwi* stew, corn-dough loaves and quinoa, wild strawberries and large, juicy cherimoyas. Bowls of *aca* were still being passed around, and now it was time to listen to Uncle Turu and his stories.

"Before I begin," Uncle Turu said, "there is one last planting task before us." Groans of disappointment sounded around the fire. What work could there be tonight? Now was the time to sit and relax and listen.

Yawar stood, and though I was sitting at the edge of the group as always, I could still see his eyes dancing in the flickering flames as he announced, "Planting isn't easy work."

The people agreed, nodding their heads and grunting, "*Ari, ari.*"

"It requires the energy of all the people, and it is a sacred task that honors the gods."

More nods of agreement — and looks of confusion. Why say these obvious things now?

"And so, when a member of our *llaqta*, our village, doesn't do his share of the work, the entire village suffers. The gods may be angered. The safety of the people is threatened. We all know the most basic rules: Do not lie, do not steal, do not be lazy."

Yawar gestured behind him, and two of the older boys ceremoniously brought forward a large bowl, carrying it between them, and set it down.

"It is time to wash our feet," Yawar stated.

I didn't understand, but some of the elders seemed to know what was happening. And one of them, a man named Sutic, began to shriek. "Oh, no! I already told you, I wasn't sleeping! I was praying to Inti with my eyes closed. Why don't you believe me?"

"Sutic, you were snoring. We could all hear," Uncle Turu said with a bemused expression.

Several of the men held Sutic down as the people filed by the bowl, dipping their feet, dirty from the work in the fields, into it one by one.

"Papa," I whispered, moving next to him in the line. "What is happening?"

"Ah, Daughter, it has been a long time since anyone

in the village has been judged guilty of so horrible a crime. Sutic was caught sleeping in the field when he should have been toiling with the rest of us. He has been warned before. Now he will learn." Papa waved a clenched fist in the air, but a smile whispered on his lips, and he made no attempt to conceal the delight in his voice.

By the time I dipped my feet into the water, it was so dark and murky, my skin was dirtier than before I had washed. The unforgiving night air enveloped my toes, turning them cold and uncomfortable. I quickly made my way back to the edge of the fire, wrapping myself tightly in my woolen cloak. Sumac sat on my shoulder, as always. I pressed the tip of my nose into his feathered belly for further warmth.

All this time, Sutic hadn't stopped his howling. Now, kicking and writhing, he was brought before Yawar.

"Sutic, you are guilty of endangering the people with your lazy ways," Yawar announced in a loud voice. "To atone for this crime, you will drink the water that cleansed us from our labors."

Now there were shrieks from the people around the fire, but these were shrieks of excitement. Sumac's claws dug more tightly into my shoulder. He was agitated by the noise and began swaying left and right. I put my hand on his head to calm him.

"Drink it, Sutic! Get your first *taste* of hard work!" Papa said, clearly amused by his wordplay.

Papa was not known for his hard-working ways. He could easily suffer Sutic's fate if he wasn't careful, but he seemed unaware of this as he slapped his knee and laughed with those around him. I thought of quiet Hatun, my older brother, slaving away on the distant roads. He was so different from our father. I admit I judged Papa poorly for his actions. I didn't understand then what I realize now: Papa was frightened that fingers would someday point in *his* direction. His jokes and loud noises hid any such fears well.

Sutic's eyes darted here and there like those of a cornered rabbit. Yawar stood next to him, his expression fierce. He would not let Sutic escape.

In one final attempt, Sutic pleaded with the crowd. "Please. I won't do it again. I have gotten a bit old, you see."

This was true. Sutic's back stooped. The lines on his face spoke of many years of laughter and sorrow. He wasn't far from the age when planting wouldn't be expected of him any longer. For a moment I wondered if the people might make me drink the dirty water as well, since my body was disfigured like Sutic's. I studied the crowd for signs that I would be joining the old man. But the people's eyes were only on him.

Ucho and his group crouched on the other side of the flames, grasping their sides in laughter and pointing at the frightened man. Chasca and Mama sat together. Mama's arm rested casually around her beautiful daughter's back.

Yawar held up the bowl of filthy water and handed it to the old man. Sutic's hands were trembling, and some of the water sloshed over the sides and onto his cloak. Slowly, he struggled to raise the bowl to his lips. To the calls and laughter of the people, Sutic tilted the bowl back and drank. His throat bobbed as he swallowed and swallowed. Long before he emptied the bowl, he fell to the ground, retching horribly.

The people were still laughing as Cora, Sutic's wife, silently made her way to him and helped him rise. Rubbing his shoulders, she led him toward their *wasi,* Sutic leaning heavily on her for support. Cora looked back longingly as Uncle Turu stood once more before the fire, and I understood. I, too, would be sorry to miss Uncle Turu's stories on a night such as this.

"Ñawpa pachapi, once upon a time, there were three brothers living with their parents." There were many sighs of contentment. Uncle Turu always told this tale after we planted, in honor of the sacred corn and Pachamama.

"It was the time of the corn harvest, and it was the oldest brother's duty to guard the family's bountiful fields. But he was newly a man and did not always take his job seriously. Each night, he would rest his eyes when he should have been watching, and cobs of corn would mysteriously disappear. Each morning, his mother would screech and scold him for being so lazy." Uncle Turu paused, allowing the word *lazy* to hang in the air and echo in the minds of the people. There were quiet chuckles throughout the crowd. More than one person mimed Sutic retching on the ground.

"Finally, the brother vowed he would stay up all night long to capture the thief. That evening, he didn't wear his warm wrap, so that the cold would keep him alert. Crouching behind a field rock, he waited. And waited. The night was silent and long, and still the brother waited." Uncle Turu paused and let the cold quiet of the night air play its part in his story. Then he went on. "As Mama Killa rested full in the night sky, some of her children, the stars, descended to the earth in the form of beautiful women with long, golden-white hair. As the brother watched, the star women floated into the corn fields and began to feast on the ripe corn.

"At first the brother didn't know what to do. He was unprepared for such a sight. But the beauty of the star women was more than he could resist. In a mad rush, he pounced on the nearest one, grabbing her by the arm. She watched sadly as her sisters vanished into the night sky, leaving her alone with the young man, a cob of corn still clutched in her delicate hand."

Uncle Turu's voice dropped to a whisper. I leaned in more closely to hear the words spoken by the star woman.

"'Please,' she said in a musical voice, 'let me go.' She stared at him with sparkling eyes as her golden-white hair blew here and there in the night breeze.

"The brother was young enough to be foolish still. 'I won't let you go,' he said. 'You have stolen from me.'

"Her lovely round face was pale in the moonlight. 'Yes,' she said. 'Let us talk.'

"And so they talked. As punishment for her crime, the star woman agreed to live with the brother. She held up the stolen corn. 'I can feed you forever with just this one cob of corn,' she whispered, 'but only if you honor two conditions: You must tell no one where I come from, and you must never look into my *manca*, my cooking pot.'

"The brother agreed. He built them a *wasi* not too far from his parents' home, and he and the star woman lived together happily. Much time passed. Every day, she would serve him the finest white corn boiled in sweet water from the lagoon. He didn't know how she fed him day after day and night after night from the same cob of corn, but he was full and content.

"The brother's mother, however, was far from happy. Without her permission, her son had moved in with a strange, golden-haired woman. He often bragged of the fine white corn they ate every day. Where did it come from? And why did he never offer to share it with his family? It wasn't proper for a son to keep the best food for himself.

"The mother decided it was time to set things right and true. One day she visited her son's *wasi*. He was sitting outside, enjoying Inti's warmth.

"'Mama,' he said, 'what a wonderful surprise. My wife is at the lagoon, but when she returns, we will eat. You must join us.'

"The mother hadn't expected such an invitation and was pleased. Still, she had questions, and she was not to be distracted. She began asking her son about his strange woman and where their corn came from. At first the son was strong and refused to answer his mother. But she continued to nag at him until, finally, he revealed the secret agreement he had made with the star woman never to look into her cooking pot. He made his mother promise not to tell anyone of the secret.

"'Of course, my son. Now, why don't you go get this woman of yours, and we can feast together as a family,' she said slyly.

"As soon as her son had gone, the mother went inside the *wasi*. There on the fiery stones of the hearth was a *manca,* hot and bubbling. Carefully, the mother lifted the lid and looked inside. Three small kernels sat in the boiling water. Only three kernels! How could this be?

"The mother went outside just in time to greet her son and the star woman returning from the lagoon. The star woman offered a quiet, shimmering smile to the mother. 'Let us eat together,' she said. They entered the *wasi*, and the star woman walked to her pot. When she looked inside, instead of a steaming heap of fine white corn, she saw only three lone kernels, the ones she had placed in the pot day after day.

"The star woman knew she had been betrayed. With tears in her eyes she said, 'It is time for me to go.' She ran straight toward the lagoon, with the brother following closely behind, screaming for her to come back.

"'Stop!' he yelled after her. 'You will drown!'

"But she didn't stop, and here an amazing sight was seen. The star woman appeared to both sink into the lagoon and rise up into the sky at the same time. The brother knew then that he had lost his star woman forever, and he was fiercely sad.

"Soon after, the brother found the cob of corn the star woman had stolen from him so long before. It was missing only three kernels. In her honor, the brother planted all the remaining kernels, and it is said that the finest white corn grew from them. This is how white corn came to be on earth, in honor of the star woman and her beautiful golden-white hair. It is also said that the mother ran away in shame and that the brother joined the star woman in the sky when he died. So it was and ever shall be."

"So it was and ever shall be," we chanted together.

Papa yelled out, "And that's why we men should never, never look into a woman's cooking pot." Papa wasn't the only man who was afraid to look into his wife's *manca*. Many of the men felt it was bad luck to do so. There were nods of agreement and snorts of enjoyment. The *aca* was all gone, but the laughter it brought was still present in many of the people.

Uncle Turu smiled and moved away from the fire. The people groaned in disappointment.

"One more!" they cajoled. "Just one more story, Turu!"

Pleased, Uncle Turu resumed his place in front of the people. "Which should I tell?" he asked, stroking his chin with his fingers.

Ucho's voice rose from the crowd. "How about the one in which the lady marries a condor?" He and his group snickered, and several of the boys looked my way.

In this story, a condor falls in love with a lady and tricks her into becoming his wife. She has to live up high in his nest, dirty and ragged, eating rotten meat.

Sumac was asleep on my shoulder, his head turned around so his beak rested in the downy softness of his back. He was a handsome bird and didn't eat meat of any kind. He also was not my husband, but this wouldn't matter to Ucho. I stood quietly and moved away from the fire. I was sorry to leave. The story was one of Uncle Turu's favorites. He liked to stretch his arms in condor flight and then wrap them around his body to become the poor woman huddled in a cold, shivering ball.

"Where are you and your bird husband going, Ugly One?" Ucho hissed after me. No one else noticed or turned. Such was Ucho's power over me, that his words could push me away from the one place where I could be truly happy. I didn't look back, but I could hear Uncle Turu's sure voice, already captivating the people. "*Ñawpa pachapi,* once upon a time . . ."

8
YACHACHISQA
Learning Girl

THE time of the first rains arrived, but still Inti beat his golden rays down upon the hard, dry earth. No shoots showed from the fields where we had planted, and the people were restless and irritable. Some carried a look of quiet worry on their faces. Some whispered that soon the very stones would explode with the heat, that we would all go hungry. Boys who should have been covered in wolf skins, protecting the new growth from hungry animals, had nothing to guard.

Ucho sat in the center of the village with his younger brother, Muti, teaching him the complicated game of *conkana*. They kneeled over the board, and Muti threw the wooden dice and moved his colored bean with a sly smile on his face. Ucho pretended to scowl, but he also put his hand on Muti's shoulder in proud support. Seeing Ucho make this small gesture of kindness and caring somehow hurt me more than any of his harsh words ever had.

Mother had asked me to collect some plants for dyeing, and I wanted to ask her a question before leaving. I shouldn't have walked through the village to find her. I should have walked around the outside. And I certainly shouldn't have paused to watch the boys playing their game.

Of course Ucho sighted me there with Sumac perched proudly on my shoulder. Sumac was still young, but his feathers were bright and bold now, and he surveyed the world with the air of a fine nobleman.

"It's the Ugly One and her filthy bird husband," Ucho said as he rose from the game. He strode quickly to us, Muti following right behind. "Perhaps I'll get you some rotting meat so you can have a proper feast."

Ucho squinted and moved closer to Sumac. The Handsome One crouched low on my shoulder and swayed slowly from side to side. His beak opened, and he made a sharp hissing sound, as if in warning. I had never seen him behave this way.

"Filthy pest!" Ucho said, and he poked a finger into Sumac's beautiful red belly.

Old Sutic, who had been dozing against a wall

nearby, stood as if to intervene, but before he could say a word, the Handsome One took action.

With a loud squawk, the bird lunged at Ucho and grabbed hold of his nose with his strong beak. Blood spurted, and Ucho screamed in anger and surprise while Sumac held on with fierce determination. With one hand, Ucho clutched at his bleeding nose. With the other he grasped for the bird, who squawked once more and took off into the air. It was his first flight, and he wobbled unsteadily as he rose higher and veered to the left. I think he was as surprised as I was to find himself flying.

I pushed past Ucho, trying to stay beneath Sumac's flight path so I wouldn't lose him. I was frightened. What if he soared so high, he couldn't come back down? What if he became lost in the mountains? He wouldn't know how to care for himself. And I would be alone again.

I need not have worried. At the outskirts of the village, Sumac slowed his flight and skidded to a landing outside the great Paqo's *wasi*. Then, looking pleased with himself, he puffed out his feathers, gave a great *braaawk,* and waddled into the Paqo's home as if he were a welcome and expected guest.

I hesitated outside. Sumac seemed uninjured, but I didn't think the Paqo would appreciate his intrusion.

Carefully, I slid past the hummingbird weaving into the *wasi,* hoping I wouldn't be interrupting an important ceremony.

The Paqo sat on the ground with Sumac perched on his arm. As he wiped Sumac's beak, which showed traces of red from his attack on Ucho, the shaman smiled and nodded his head, and I was struck by the feeling that the two of them were having a true conversation. There was a familiarity in their movements that made me wonder if Sumac had visited the Paqo before, without my knowledge.

"Don't worry. Ucho will be fine. I'll treat him when he comes to me later," the Paqo said, and I wasn't sure if he was talking to me or to Sumac.

"I don't think Ucho will ever be fine," I muttered.

The Paqo looked up with a bemused expression, but it was to Sumac that he spoke. "So she *does* have a voice."

Sumac bobbed his head up and down. He did this often to show he was pleased with himself, but now it looked as if he was agreeing with the shaman. The Paqo cocked his head at the bird. "Perhaps. We shall see." Sumac spread his wings and flew over to me. His claws curled into my shoulder reassuringly as he landed, his bird body a welcome weight.

"Ucho is cruel," I said hotly. And then I spewed forth

feelings I hadn't shared before with anyone. "He is very cruel. I would stomp him into the ground if I could. I would feed him to the serpents. I would tie him to a rock for many days and nights and listen to him cry out for water, and I wouldn't move to help. Not at all."

The Paqo replied in a tone that was much calmer than mine. "All creatures serve a purpose. If it weren't for the boy, you wouldn't be here now, speaking your mind, showing you have thoughts other than how to hide. He has given you courage."

I spoke more quietly now. "He is the reason I hide."

"Ah. There is strength in this new voice of yours. But it lacks wisdom."

The Paqo's comment made me bristle. I believed he was wrong, for I thought myself wiser than most. But I wasn't about to argue with this powerful man.

The Paqo stood and joined me, pulling aside the door weaving to reveal the trees outside. "Learn the lessons hidden in the leaves."

This was riddle talk I didn't understand, so I said nothing.

"See how the wind blows the tree?" he went on, pointing to a young *molle*. "Do the leaves fight the wind? Of course not. Are they angry because it moves them back and forth? No. Does the wind change the

nature of the leaf? Not at all. The leaf *is*. Y[
lowed the wind to change your nature."

I didn't care much then about the le[
wind. "But Ucho stings at me all the time. I am tired o[
it."

"We all have our troubles. Cruel words. No rain." I
couldn't tell if the shaman was mocking me. "You have
chosen your way."

"I never chose this!"

His face softened. "No. No, you did not," he said
gently, staring at my right cheek. "But you choose to
fight what is."

The wind shifted direction. With it, a sense of unease filled my chest.

"They are coming for the bird," the shaman said.

These words immediately filled me with fear. Of
course they were coming for Sumac. He had bitten
Ucho. They would kill my beautiful bird, my one true
friend. My entire body began to tremble. What was I to
do?

"He attacked a member of the *llaqta*," the Paqo
stated.

"Ucho attacked him first."

"The bird is a menace."

My shaking stopped at this accusation. Here I met

the Paqo's gaze and held it firmly in my own. "You know he is not."

The shaman smiled fully, the gap in his top front teeth a message of enjoyment. "You presume to tell the great Paqo what he does or does not know?"

It was because of the smile that I was able to reply, "Yes."

"They will see the bird as a threat. Does this not make him a threat?"

"I don't know how to answer your questions. You speak in riddles that I don't understand."

"Ah! The new voice speaks first with strength and now with wisdom. I will discuss the matter with Yawar. It is time for you to leave, for soon they will arrive with the injured boy."

I nodded. It wouldn't be safe for Sumac if Ucho and the others found us now. Better to hide and let hot tempers cool.

As I turned to flee, the shaman chuckled. "So you see? You came when the bird told you to," he said.

Sumac squawked and bobbed his head up and down once more in agreement, as if the two of them had conspired to bring me there.

"You will come back tomorrow."

"I will?"

"Yes. There are many hidden lessons waiting to be

seen and heard and felt. They want to be understood. I will reveal them to you."

I had no time to reply. As I slipped away between the trees and branches, careful to avoid the path of the people, my head was busy with fierce wonderings. How could the Paqo have known what had happened? I had not told him that Sumac had bitten Ucho, yet the shaman was clearly aware of the attack. I eyed Sumac warily. Exactly how much had he shared with the great Paqo? But these questions were tiny pebbles compared with my mountainous wonder at what had just happened. I was fairly certain that I had become the apprentice of the great Paqo.

◙◙

I stayed away until it was time for the evening meal. The moment I entered the *wasi,* Father put down his bowl of stew and began screeching. "Where have you been? Yawar was here looking for you! You have shamed us all with that creature of yours!"

Mama studied Sumac atop my shoulder. "Will they kill the bird?" she asked quietly.

"I don't think so. The Paqo said he would speak on my behalf." I took my place on the floor and poured a bowl of stew for myself.

"Why would he do that?" Chasca asked.

A worthwhile question. I was uncertain of the true

reason, so I offered the simplest explanation. "I am to study with him."

The entire family went silent at this.

"You are to study with the great Paqo? Such an honor! How did this happen? What spirits smile upon us to bring such good fortune?" Papa was clearly pleased. He viewed the world with an eye for status and power. I smiled, glad that I had made him proud.

"Are you sure this is wise?" Chasca asked in concern. "I have heard he is disgraced, that he was sent away from Cuzco by the Sapa Inca himself."

I had heard this as well. It was the favored explanation for the Paqo's sudden arrival in our *llaqta* several years ago. But even if I had been frightened by such sayings, I couldn't have denied the mighty shaman. He had chosen me. I was to study with him.

Mama smiled at me and said, "We don't know why the Paqo left the capital city, but I am certain he has much to teach you. You will be a good *yachachisqa,* a strong learning girl. Just be careful, my daughter."

It is these last words that showed Mama's right and true heart. She was afraid. But I didn't ask myself then what it was that brought fear to my quiet, watching mother. It didn't occur to me until later that dwelling in the realm of the spirits could bring danger, especially to an ugly girl in a time when the rains didn't come.

9
MUSUQ SIMI
New Voice

THE next morning, Sumac and I went to the Paqo's *wasi* after the morning sun greeting. He already had a visitor: Cora, the unfortunate wife of old Sutic. He gestured me inside, and I seated myself beside them without speaking.

The Paqo was studying the inside of a large clay jar. I peered in and saw a handful of spiders crawling about. The hearth fire crackled and hissed as he slowly waved his fingers and whispered strangely to the spiders. "Yes, yes. I see. But what of the back?"

Cora sat with wide eyes, her hands clenched tightly in worry. The Paqo leaned in so closely, his lips almost touched the edge of the jar. He smiled down on the scurrying eight-legged creatures and whispered, "Ah, yes. To the right. I see." Then he sat up abruptly and spoke to Cora. "Your husband will sleep on his right side. This will help the back pain. Be sure he takes the medicines."

Cora opened her hands to examine a small pouch she held. She nodded her head vigorously. "*Pachis*, thank you, mighty shaman. *Pachis*!"

The Paqo selected a cluster of dried grasses hanging upside down from the roof beam. "This is *muña* grass," he said as he handed it to her. "Burn it inside the *wasi*. Breathe in the smoke. It will help soothe your headaches."

Cora looked at him in surprise, and I could see she hadn't told him of her own physical pains.

"It isn't always so easy to be the wife of Sutic, eh?" the Paqo asked with a gentle smile. Cora smiled back at him uncertainly and gave a faint nod of agreement. She studied the *muña* with wonder before delicately placing it inside the folds of her clothing.

I had never thought much about Cora's troubles before. I had seen her my whole life, and not once had I asked myself what it would be like to be her. To watch her husband retch up filthy foot water in front of the people, to stand by his side while others laughed, to support him and walk away from Uncle Turu and his stories. None of this could have been easy. How many similar moments had she experienced? Was it possible she was as unhappy in life as I was?

Rising, Cora kissed her fingers and bowed toward the Paqo. She slowly backed her way out of the *wasi*, pausing to bow and kiss her fingers every few steps. Then, with a final *"Pachis!"* she was gone. I hoped the medicines would help her husband's stooping back and her aching head. I wondered if I might learn something that could help her. And then it occurred to me that there might come a time when the Paqo would use his power to heal my scarred face. Might I ever have the courage to ask him to do such a thing?

"You are free to go," the Paqo said.

At first I thought he meant me, but then I saw the spiders were leaving the jar, crawling over the thick edge and down toward the earth to safety. One lone spider remained atop the jar, its delicate legs blending in to the thin geometric designs that crisscrossed their way down the painted sides.

"Will the new voice speak today?"

I smiled. I was nervous. I didn't know why I was there or what we would do. More talk of the lessons in the leaves, perhaps? "Yes," I said.

The Paqo scowled. "No," he replied. "Today the new voice listens."

Even simple questions were not to be answered lightly in this place. My first word of the lesson, and it was wrong. I repeated, "Today the new voice listens."

The Paqo nodded with a quiet grunt of affirmation. And then he said nothing. For a long time, he sat and said nothing. I stayed seated as well, waiting for his next words. They didn't come. Still I didn't speak. I would not be wrong again. If I must, I would wait all day for his words.

Sumac rested comfortably, his cheek next to my head. He tucked his left leg up to his belly and began grating the top and bottom of his beak together, a quiet sound that told me he was preparing to sleep. It soothed me somewhat, but I felt now that I was somehow failing to solve a simple riddle. What did the Paqo want me to do? Why had he chosen me to study with him when I couldn't answer even the easiest of questions? I should leave. I wasn't meant to be here. Not only was I ugly, I was unwise. It was a terrible thing to realize about myself, for what did I have left?

"Well?" the Paqo asked sharply. "What did you hear?"

And suddenly I understood. I was supposed to have been listening not to the Paqo's words but to something else. What had I heard? In a panic,

I tried to grasp at some sound. "Sumac falling asleep."

"And what is the sound of a bird falling asleep?"

"He grates his beak. The sound grows louder, then slows and stops. When he is quiet, I know he has fallen asleep."

"You didn't see him fall asleep," the Paqo said. This was a statement, not a question, for he had been watching me the whole time and knew it was so. "Are you certain he is truly sleeping?"

"Yes."

"How?"

I didn't turn to look at Sumac. Instead, I kept my gaze on the Paqo. "I know. He is standing on one foot as he does in sleep. I can feel it in the way he grips my shoulder. He is very still."

The Paqo smiled. "Good. Very good. Now study the spider."

Perhaps I had passed the listening test. I turned my attention to the lone spider still sitting atop the jug. It was motionless, but Sumac stirred in response to my subtle shift in position.

"All is one. All is now," the Paqo said. "To realize this is to reach Beyond. Study the spider. Learn its wisdom. Its eyes are your eyes. All is one. There is a language more powerful and ancient than the human tongue. Hear the language of the world."

I tried to understand. I leaned forward, watching the spider so intently, my eyes began to water and blur. Still I stared. I tried to listen to the wisdom of the spider.

Suddenly, Sumac reached down, and in one quick peck he snatched the bug into his mouth. The Handsome One had eaten my spider lesson!

The Paqo hooted with laughter. He rubbed his head in delight. "You see? Again the bird is a teacher! Where is the spider? Has it disappeared?"

"It's in there now," I said as I pointed to Sumac's belly. He stretched his wings upward and bobbed his feathered head in bird delight.

"We all are one. Bird and spider. Leaf and wind. To hear is to see. To feel is to know. The past is now. All is Beyond. Do you understand?"

Another question. I would answer truthfully. "No."

The Paqo nodded his head appreciatively at my honesty. "Good. Then you are not meant to."

I wasn't meant to understand? Then why was I here? Was this to be my last lesson?

The Paqo twitched his fingers at me as he added, "Yet."

I was afraid to speak, but also, I was afraid not to.

"Will there come a time when I *do* understand? Is it possible I am the right and true person to study with you?"

"I'm not the one to answer such questions."

"Who is?"

"You."

The word hovered in the air. It clung to my wool cloak and settled on my shoulders far more heavily than the weight of Sumac.

"But not yet," the Paqo added. "New voices need time to grow. Study the spiders. Study all. Watch, listen, feel the oneness. You will know when you will know."

This was the end of the lesson. I didn't back out of the *wasi* bowing and kissing my fingers at the Paqo as Cora had, for it didn't seem appropriate. But I did pause at the hummingbird weaving in the doorway to say, *"Pachis."*

"You are most welcome, New Voice. I will see you tomorrow."

I smiled at these words. Not only because they told me there would be more lessons, but also because I had finally been given a name other than the Ugly One.

10
MAMA KILLA
Moon Mother

I studied all. I watched the people purge their homes at the start of the new moon. Every corner was cleaned, and corn-dough was rubbed along entranceways to appease the spirits of dirt and sickness. I listened for the ancient language of the world as Mama Killa, Moon Mother, grew larger in the sky night by night, but I had yet to hear the voice of Beyond right and true. I found myself questioning more and more why the shaman had chosen me. The spirit world would never speak to such an ugly girl, no matter how hard or long I listened.

I heard the laughter of the women and the girls of the *llaqta*. Not because the rains had arrived, for Inti still reigned in the daytime skies, but because it was Coya Raymi, a time of celebration for the women. It was during this moon cycle, once a year, that the women and Mama Killa were most honored and happy. On the night when Mama Killa was at her fullest, the entire village celebrated with a lavish communal meal, although no one spoke of how meager the feast would be this year. I studied the people and saw the worry carved into their faces like a carefully designed mask.

A strange shift had occurred in me. But I was so intent on studying the world that I didn't notice it until Chasca pointed it out to me. It was the night of the full moon. We sat together by the fire, waiting for Uncle Turu to begin his storytelling.

"You are changing," Chasca said, her skin glowing a beautiful gold in the firelight.

"I am?"

"Yes. You have never sat with me by the fire before."

"You are right!" I said in surprise.

Chasca smiled and put her arm around my back. She rested her head lightly on my left shoulder. Sumac preened himself happily on the other side, and I will say I felt as full and content as Mama Killa at that moment.

Chasca had spoken truly. As you have heard, I always sat away from the people, at the edge of the group. This was a small observation she had made, but also not so small. I wondered what was different.

I often forgot myself in my watching and listening.

I had been studying the flames of the fire when Chasca spoke to me. But there was another reason, and I thought I knew what it was as I sat with my beautiful sister. The people treated me differently. They smiled my way more often.

Some of these smiles were fearful. They were tight lipped, with nervous, flitting eyes. These people were afraid of my powers as the *yachachisqa*, the student of the mighty shaman, or perhaps they were scared of Sumac and his big beak. But other smiles were wide and true. These smiles came for a reason that is difficult to explain. Imagine a girl rushing through her days with her head down, her face hidden behind her hair. Would you grin at such a girl as she scuttled past you in fear? No. Now see this same girl moving slowly, watching you. She will see your smile, yes? So you offer it to her.

By opening my eyes and my ears, I was creating a world of more smiles for myself. It was an odd and new sensation, to be seen after a lifetime spent feeling as invisible as the very air, and I was still learning to return those smiles.

One person in particular, Ucho, had changed his ways toward me as quickly as the air turns frigid once Inti sets from the sky. Ucho ignored me completely now. As I reflected on it by the fire, I realized that I hadn't seen him much over the past moon. I searched the faces and found him on the opposite side of the fire, sitting with his brother and the other boys. His nose had healed, but it would always have a strange twisted appearance at the end. Perhaps it wasn't me that Ucho avoided, but the Handsome One. I decided it didn't much matter, as long as he stayed away.

Sighing happily, I rested my head against Chasca's as Uncle Turu stepped in front of the fire. Tonight would be one of the people's favorite stories, a love story, that always sparked much debate after its telling.

Uncle Turu rose, rubbing his big hands together briskly in expectation. He waited for the people to grow quiet before beginning. When the air was heavy with the silence of the surrounding mountains and every pair of eyes was fixed intently on him, Uncle Turu boomed, *"Ñawpa pachapi."*

There is much power in these opening words, yes? Can you see the people settling onto the earth more comfortably, content to be caught up in the story Uncle Turu would weave for them?

"Once upon a time there was a girl named Chuguillanto who was more beautiful than any across the empire. She hadn't a single freckle or mole, and her face was so perfect, the very birds stopped their singing when she walked by, for she was far lovelier than any song they could offer.

"When she was eight, Chuguillanto was selected to become a member of the Acllahuasi, the convent of the Sun Maidens, in the capital city of Cuzco. Most of the Sun Maidens would become wives to noblemen, or servants to the sacred mummies, or weavers of the finest cloth worn by the Sapa Inca. But such was not to be the fate of Chuguillanto. Because of her great beauty, the emperor himself had chosen her to be the next offering to Inti if the times demanded a human sacrifice. In a convent of thousands of Sun Maidens, such a selection was the greatest of honors.

"Life in the convent was very, very good. The Maidens ate the finest of delicacies the land could provide, served upon plates of ornately carved gold. They slept on raised beds filled with the soft wool of baby alpacas. Their clothes were woven of richly dyed cloths and adorned with beautiful feathers and shells. Four mighty fountains flowed forth from the four corners of the empire, so that each Maiden might bathe herself in waters from her home province. It is said that such waters helped to maintain the beauty and softness of the skin." Here Uncle Turu fluttered his eyes and delicately rubbed his cheek with his fingers, and the people laughed to see such a strong-faced man pretending to be beautiful.

"Of course the Sun Maidens' hearts had to be pure.

They couldn't attend to their duties properly if they didn't devote themselves entirely to the emperor and to Inti. So they were carefully guarded. Maidens were allowed to leave the convent only in pairs, and they were questioned and inspected upon their return for hidden mementos or charms, a sure sign that a Maiden had allowed herself to fall in love with a man. Such a Maiden would be buried alive for turning her heart elsewhere.

"Several years passed, and Chuguillanto became known as the most beautiful young woman in all the empire. One day she and another Sun Maiden wandered far from the convent and came across a handsome young herdsman napping under a tree, his llamas grazing on the *ichu* grass. As the Maidens approached, the scent of their perfume awoke the youth. When he saw them, he scrambled to his feet and bowed low, for he was certain he was gazing upon goddesses.

"Chuguillanto's companion laughed and assured the herdsman that they were mortal. Chuguillanto, however, was quiet, for already the llama herder had captivated her. The other Sun Maiden asked the herdsman's name, and he told her he was called Acoynapa, but it was to Chuguillanto that he truly spoke, for he was as captivated by her as she was by him.

"The three passed the afternoon together, enjoying

one another's company. Acoynapa wore an unusual silver *campu,* a pendant, on a thin silver chain about his forehead. Chuguillanto asked to see it, and when Acoynapa leaned closer toward her so she could do so, they both were overcome by the closeness and pulled away quickly.

"Acoynapa offered the pendant to Chuguillanto as a gift, but she refused, for she knew if the guards discovered it, she would be slain. Acoynapa would be in danger as well. If he was found guilty of capturing a Sun Maiden's heart, he would be hung from his feet until the blood rushing to his head made it burst from the pressure." Here Uncle Turu placed his hands on the sides of his head and pulled the hair away from his face, grimacing horribly. He paused to let the image sink in, then went on with the story.

"Back in the Acllahuasi that night, Chuguillanto tossed about, unable to sleep, for she was in love with the llama herder. Although she was a wise and sensible girl, she resolved to find his home and see him again. Acoynapa also didn't sleep that night, for he, too, had fallen in love and knew the terrible consequences if he should be found out.

"The week that followed was full of suffering for the pair. Chuguillanto wandered the hills with her companion, going from home to home looking for Acoynapa. Acoynapa lay in his *wasi*, unable to sleep or eat. Finally, his mother came to visit him. When she saw the state her son was in, she knew he would die from his lovesickness if she didn't help. Fortunately, she was a woman of much magic. She shrank her eager son and placed him inside a finely carved wooden staff.

"The day arrived when Chuguillanto and her companion knocked on the door of Acoynapa's home. The mother answered and told the Maidens that Acoynapa had died. She handed Chuguillanto the wooden staff, saying it had been his favorite and she should take it as a way to remember him. Chuguillanto thanked the mother and, clutching the staff to her chest, walked back to the convent with her companion. The guards allowed the staff inside, for it wasn't concealed and was the property of a dead man who could be no threat.

"That night, Chuguillanto placed the wooden staff in her room and began sobbing. As the tears flowed down her cheeks and landed on the staff, it began to tremble and transform right before her eyes. Suddenly, kneeling before her was her beloved herdsman! The two embraced with much joy, and Acoynapa explained about the magic powers of the staff.

"It was in this way that the two lived together in the most heavily guarded convent in the empire without being discovered. By day, Acoynapa hid himself in the staff, and Chuguillanto would walk about holding the stick close to her. At night, once they were safe within the walls of her room, he would transform into his human self.

"But, as is always the way, these good times did not last. Famine and plague struck the empire. The dead outnumbered the living, and there weren't enough hands to bury the bodies piling up in the roads."

Uncle Turu clutched his belly in hunger. He mopped his brow in fever and held his head in agony.

"The Sapa Inca consulted his wise men and was told it was time for a human sacrifice. This was to be Chuguillanto's moment. Her death would be painless. Filled with the magic of the *koka* leaves and *aca*, she wouldn't feel the fingers wrapped around her throat to stop her breath forever. She would be a messenger to Inti and dwell with him forever as a representative of her people. There was no greater glory.

"But Chuguillanto knew she was an impure sacrifice, for her heart belonged to Acoynapa. The entire empire would suffer if she was offered to the Sun God, and the Sapa Inca would be cursed. Ignorance was no excuse. She couldn't allow herself to be sacrificed, but to confess would lead to her death and that of her beloved. What could she do? She and Acoynapa devised a hasty plan. In the middle of the night, they fled to the east, hoping to be taken in by the people of the jungle.

"But their escape was not meant to be. The gods themselves intervened. As the two were about to reach the jungle, they were turned into stone pillars, one on either side of the road. Neither in the empire nor in freedom, neither together nor apart, they stand for eternity for all to see."

Uncle Turu held up his hands in a question. "Did the gods do this in honor of the great love shared by Chuguillanto and Acoynapa, or as a punishment because they broke the laws of the empire? No one is certain. So it was and ever shall be."

The people repeated, "So it was and ever shall be."

"They were turned to stone in glory!" someone yelled.

"No! The gods did it because they were insulted!" another responded. Immediately, the debating began, but it was all in good nature. Chasca and I smiled at each other. We had our own disagreement about Chuguillanto.

"She was a fool," I whispered. Chuguillanto could have been sacrificed to Inti, could have spent eternity in his constant presence. She gave this up for a mere llama herder. Chasca knew my arguments. I did not need to repeat them.

My sister answered, "She was courageous in life and lucky to be in love." Here was one of our greatest differences. Chasca preferred a man. I would choose no less than the Sun God himself if I could. I traced my jagged scar lightly with the back of my fingers. The faraway jungle was closer to me than Chuguillanto's unblemished beauty.

Chasca seemed to know my thoughts. "Come," she said. "Let's dance the *aymaran*." My sister especially enjoyed this ancient dance because of its fast spinning. Several other women were already rising to the beginning sounds of the drums. This was part of the celebration, that the women would dance without the men.

Although it is true that I was changing, I couldn't bring myself to dance with anything more than small, careful steps. Sumac clutched my shoulder, his claws digging in tightly so he wouldn't fall off. To move too quickly might expose my scarred cheek to the people, and I wasn't prepared to do that. But Chasca quickly abandoned herself to the now rapidly beating drums. Her feet flew in a quickening circle, her hair flowing in an arc behind her as she leaned her head back and reached to Mama Killa with open arms. I stopped dancing and watched, as many others did. My sister was beautiful and free and open. Mama Killa and her children, the stars, shone down on Chasca in gladness, kissing her pure, smooth skin as she laughed and twirled under their magical glow.

I left the dancers quickly, although I hesitated at the edge of the fire circle to watch. The drums beat more loudly, with a pulsing intensity. Their insistent voices converged into the one pounding sound of *dance dance dance*. But I was the Ugly One, and the *aymaran* was not meant for me. Patting Sumac on the head, I turned and made my way back to the *wasi* alone.

〰〰

That night in my dreams, I again visited the heart of my *huaca*, my spirit rock. I stood inside the cave. The air was filled with the whispers and echoes of ancient spirits, and on the rock wall I could see a faint carving of my brother Hatun's face. It was frozen in a moment of horror and fear.

Two jaguar cubs snarled at each other in play as they frolicked on the dirt floor. I thought to join them and dropped to my hands and knees. Such fun they were having! I inched my way forward, hoping they wouldn't stop their play before I could pounce on them in surprise.

A large padded foot suddenly blocked my path. It was the mother jaguar. She studied me with yellow eyes and an open mouth. I wasn't frightened of her sharp teeth, for I knew she wouldn't hurt me. Her breath was hot and animal on my face, and a delicate rainbow snaked its way slowly from deep within her throat and out past her lips. I inhaled it into my own being and held it deep within my chest, where it tingled warm and magical. I didn't want to release it, but my chest was burning for fresh air. I opened my mouth with a roar. The rainbow rushed toward the cubs in a swirl and wrapped them in its misty colors. They froze, one of them in midpounce, then dried up and quickly disappeared into the ground.

"Look," Mother Jaguar said.

Crawling closer, I studied the spot where the cubs had been. Something creamy and delicate burst forth from the dark earth and began to grow. It was a tiny, perfect toadstool.

"Soon," Mother Jaguar said. With great tenderness, she scooped up the fragile toadstool in her mouth and was gone in one mighty leap.

I awoke. The *wasi* was very dark, and I pulled my blanket tightly around my shoulders to keep out the cold air. I knew the dream was an important message, but now that I was awake, I could remember none of it. It was a gift, to have the spirits speak with me in such a manner. They honored me with their presence. To forget their message was a failure that further convinced me I was not the right and true apprentice to the shaman. I had listened, but still the voice of Beyond was silent to my straining ears. I had watched, but my eyes were blind to its sacred vision. My timid feet couldn't even dance the *aymaran*.

Lying there that night, I made a decision to follow what my heart told me was the sad but steady path. I would end my studies with the Paqo. I would tell him in the morning.

11
INTI
Sun Father

EARLY the next day, I went to my *huaca*. This was my favorite place to greet Inti each morning. As I sat there, the night's cold seeping from the rock's strong body through my thick woolen cloak, I had a vague sense that somehow the *huaca* had been a part of the dream that danced in the dark just out of memory's reach. I tried to call it forth, concentrating on the sacred stone and what it might have to say, but there was nothing. No *huaca* voice. No language from Beyond. I would visit the Paqo after the greeting to tell him of my decision.

Sumac perched erect on my shoulder as if he were standing guard, awaiting the rising of the Sun God. The remaining clouds in the sky were thin and deep red. Inti would soon show himself. I rose and held my arms to the sky. "Oh, Inti," I chanted.

"Inti, Inti, Inti," Sumac mimicked in his bird voice. He had begun copying many sounds lately, and "Inti" was the first word he had learned.

I kept my focus on the Sun God. "Great Father of the Inca. Shine glory on us in safety. Shine glory on us in peace. Shine glory on us in wisdom. Keep our minds clear in light. Keep our hearts young in warmth. Keep our feet straight on the light path, for we are your children. Inti, Inti, Great Father of the Inca."

Here I added my own personal prayer to the sun. It was perhaps selfish of me to do so, but every morning I implored, "And please, Mighty Inti, remove my scar." I knew he could do it if he so chose. But how was an ugly, scarred girl to convince the Sun God she was worthy of such attention? I kissed my fingers and bowed to the sky, the mountains silent witnesses to my worship.

The cool wind blew my hair this way and that as Inti first appeared on the horizon. I smiled at him, gladness radiating from my heart. I should have been praying for rains, yes, but the warmth of Inti's rays on my face brought me much joy. How could I ignore such happiness? It was a true mystery to me, how the Sun Maiden Chuguillanto could choose a short life with a llama herder rather than eternity with Inti. Watching his fiery body rise between the distant mountains, I could feel him in my own beating heart, spreading love throughout my chest and warming my entire being. He was our father, the most powerful of the gods. And he shone on me as if I were just as worthy as the beautiful Chuguillanto.

The greeting done, I sat to enjoy a light breakfast alone with Sumac. The moment I removed the pouch of cold cooked corn, he jumped to the ground and squawked in delight. The Handsome One favored the golden corn above all else, a sure sign he was a true bird of Inti and not of the faraway jungles. He took a kernel in his beak and ate it hungrily, flipping the soft discarded casing onto the dirt.

Mama was forever complaining about how messy Sumac was, and she had cause to grumble. While I was careful to clean up his droppings, it was difficult to capture the seed casings that he scattered across the floor. Mama also did not appreciate that Sumac was forever trying to sneak dried corn from our large storage jar. Each time she saw him waddling toward it, she would scold, "No. No. No! NO!" Each *no* was louder than the one before it, until the bird finally gave up and ran away. Lately, whenever Sumac approached the jar, he would squawk, "No. No. No! NO!" in his funny bird voice, warning Mama of his intentions even before she had noticed and could tell him to stop. He couldn't seem to help himself, even though he gave himself away every time.

"He is a horrible thief," Mama would say with a half smile.

Father was more forgiving of the bird, for he enjoyed the molted red feathers Sumac left behind. Mama had already woven some of the longer ones into Father's woolen cloak, and he strutted about like royalty whenever the opportunity presented itself. Father also appreciated one of the sounds Sumac had learned from our family. The Handsome One imitated Father's unhappy sigh perfectly, and Father enjoyed having a fellow complainer in our midst.

A piece of corn casing was stuck to the side of Sumac's beak. With a vigorous shake of his head, it flew upward and landed on my chin. I laughed. This had happened before. He took time to scratch the side of his face rapidly with his foot, then attacked the corn pile again. Sumac wasn't the most polite companion with whom to share a meal, but he was fun. I joined him, also enjoying the cold corn. I knew there were many who would judge me poorly for sharing my food with a bird in such difficult times as these, but the happiness he brought to my heart was stronger than the hunger that gnawed at my belly.

I leaned back against the rock, and Sumac jumped onto my knees. With a loud squawk, he bobbed his head and playfully nipped at the blanket I had spread across my lap. This was his favorite game. I slipped my hand under the blanket and made a bump with my fist. He studied the bump carefully, then pounced upon it with his large beak. He could have ripped through the blanket and torn my flesh if he had so chosen, but the Handsome One was always gentle with me. I moved my fist from side to side, and he lifted his blue-green wings as he held on and scolded furiously. I shook my hand and playfully punched at him through the blanket. He fluffed his feathers to show the world how mighty he was, and he attacked the blanket with all the pride he could muster. He squawked and screeched with joy and sighed loudly like Father. To see so beautiful a bird playing in such a silly manner made me laugh. But my laughter stopped abruptly when Sumac took off suddenly in flight.

He had been flying more and more frequently, but always in the past he'd done so because something had startled him, and he'd returned quickly to the ground. This was the first time he had left me without cause. I shielded my eyes from Inti's now-bright glare and followed Sumac's path. I felt as though my very heart had taken off with him. He soared higher in the sky world toward the mountaintops and Inti's home. I could not force him to return to me, so I decided to lie flat on the earth and watch as he circled in a wide arc, his wings spread like a feathered god of the skies.

It was at this point that something very unexpected happened. If you have had a similar experience, you might understand. Otherwise, I fear it will be difficult to comprehend. I'll share it with you as best I can.

As I was watching the Handsome One soaring in the sky world, it was as if I was no longer lying on the earth. Instead, I felt I was with him in the skies, flying through the air. I'm not certain if I was Sumac or myself, but I saw the earth and the mountains from his eyes as surely as if they were my own. The withered land and the people's *wasis* and the smaller mountains spread below me tiny and bound to the earth. The sharp wind flowed under and around me in a glorious rush, blowing away all sorrows from my spirit. I felt I could reach up and caress Inti himself if I chose.

Just as I realized where I was, my body was back on the ground. It happened that quickly. My breath was shallow and fast. My hands shook as I sat up. What had just happened? In a mad rush, Sumac came flapping down and landed in front of me, raising a small cloud of dust. Then he hopped lightly back onto my shoulder.

I eyed the bird. Had he done this to me? He took

a long wing feather into his beak and slowly preened himself. If he knew what had happened, he wasn't telling me. There was only one person who could. It was time to visit the Paqo.

⊡⊡

The moment I entered his *wasi,* the Paqo sat tall and said, "Tell me."

You may think it odd that I didn't ask the Paqo how he knew something had happened. Or perhaps you don't think it strange at all, for it was his way to know such things before I said a word. I rushed to his side and tried to describe my unexpected flight in the sky world. He listened with eyes that studied my every twitch and expression. "Paqo, was that Beyond?" I asked as I finished. "Did I finally visit Beyond?"

He squinted and said nothing. In the long silence, I realized he would not be offering me any simple answers.

"You aren't going to tell me, are you?" I asked.

Still he studied me.

"You're going to say that only I can know if I visited Beyond, that in my heart I should know the answer already."

He stroked his chin.

"I don't know if it was Beyond. But it was somewhere, somewhere different and filled with spirit."

He was as still as a living rock on the earth.

"I want it to happen again. I want to soar with the gods. I wonder how I did it."

A smile gleamed in the shaman's eyes, but it didn't find its way to his lips. His silence rested about him like a thick fog.

"I can do it. I can fly again. I know it's in my path." I nodded. "Thank you, Paqo. You have been most helpful."

As I was about to leave, he finally spoke. Of course, it was to ask a question, not to offer an answer. "Was there something else you wanted to tell me?"

Now it was my turn to be silent. The excitement of my flight had blown away any thoughts of ending my studies with the shaman. I had entirely forgotten my decision of the night before. I grinned. "No, Paqo. I have nothing else to say."

"Good," he said. He raised his finger pretending to scold me. "This new voice of yours rambles on like thunder in the rainy season."

"Yes, Paqo."

"It is because you released yourself from expectation that you visited the sky world. Remain open to all, New Voice. The world will give you what is right and true, but it is rarely what you expect it to be."

"Thank you, Paqo."

Walking back to my family's *wasi,* I questioned the wisdom of the shaman. I would try to stay open to what came my way, but I wasn't convinced that the world would give me what was right and true. In fact, such an idea angered me. Yes, I had flown in the sky and it had been wonderful. But what could be right and true about scarring a girl for life?

12
YANAPA

Helping

THE Paqo slowly began teaching me the ways of the herbs and spirits to heal the people. I felt a growing comfort with the magic of the plants and the animals and the gods, as if we were becoming true friends, but I didn't think the people would ever allow me to heal them. Who would agree to have the Ugly One speak to the spirits for him? Who would want the Loathsome One to touch her body? How could I be a healer right and true if I had no one to heal? Every time one of the people came to the Paqo, he would ask me if I was ready to help. I would see the person, in discomfort or pain already, eyeing me warily, and I would tell my teacher no, I was not yet ready. He would nod his head and work his ways while I watched from the side.

I told Mama of my worries. She tried to reassure

me, but still when the people came to the Paqo with their troubles and ailments, I held back, afraid that they would reject me.

Then, late one afternoon while I was studying the messages of the spiders with my teacher, Mama herself came to his *wasi* in need of healing. She entered almost apologetically and said, "I'm so sorry to interrupt such important lessons, but I burned my hand preparing the evening meal." She glanced at me and offered one of her Mama smiles.

"New Voice, are you ready to help?" the Paqo asked, as he always did now.

Before I could reply, Mama said, "I insist that she does."

My teacher smiled and stepped back. I trembled like a baby leaf fluttering in the wind as I moved toward my mother. What if I made a mistake? Mama deserved to be healed right and true. I took her hand in my own and studied it. The burn wasn't severe. I knew what to do. Carefully, tenderly, with the Paqo watching, I ground up the proper plants, added water, and made a cool poultice to apply to Mama's burnt skin, all the while speaking to the spirits of the plants, asking them to work their magic. Mama held still, a proud smile on her lips the entire time.

"We are done for now," I said. My voice was quieter than I would have liked, but it was sure and steady. "I can make you a fresh poultice tomorrow and every day after that until the skin has healed."

Mama rose. She bowed and kissed her fingers as she said, "*Pachis*," then left the *wasi*. Her movements were so graceful, it was hard to understand how she could have burned herself.

I watched Mama and her hand carefully over the following days, and I thanked Inti when the skin healed without scarring. Papa bragged to everyone in the village of his skillful daughter. Mama proudly showed her hand to all who asked, as if she were showing off a new piece of fine jewelry. And this is how the people came to accept me when they needed relief from their troubles.

Cora, old Sutic's wife, came to me for the *muña* grass to relieve her headaches. I spoke to the spiders on behalf of old Sutic and gave him medicines for his back pain. Helping the people felt good. I found the confidence to speak my words, and they listened to me. I wasn't silent or invisible as I had once been. I found myself reaching out to others, even when I wasn't in the Paqo's *wasi*.

When I saw old Sutic asleep on the earth, leaning

against a tree when he should have been working, I nudged him awake. I tried to rouse him and get him to finish his work, but it was obvious he couldn't do it, so I helped him stand and told him I would assist him home. Sumac flew off to the sky world to make room for the old man to lean on my shoulder. I could feel his bones through my wrap as I supported him, and we shuffled slowly along the dusty path. I was thankful no one saw us. He needed to rest, not to be told to go back to work.

When we reached his *wasi,* Cora took his arm onto her own shoulders. "Some nights the pain in his back keeps him from sleeping," she explained with some embarrassment, and as she stood there, stooped under the weight of her husband, I could see from the darkness below her eyes that Sutic wasn't the only one being kept awake by his aches. "Thank you for bringing him home," she added, and I nodded, wishing I could do more for them both.

A much more challenging person arrived at the Paqo's *wasi* in need of help. Nayaraq, Ucho's mother, came to us carrying her younger son, Muti, in her arms. Muti was howling in pain. Ucho followed close behind with a fierce frown on his face. Nayaraq placed Muti on the floor before us and raised her voice to be heard over her son's loud cries. "These two boys! I told them not to play so roughly. Ucho, he wasn't careful, and now look!" She pointed to Muti's shoulder, which was hanging strangely.

"The shoulder is dislocated," the Paqo said. "New Voice, hold on to his body while I manipulate it."

"No!" Ucho screamed. "The Loathsome One will not heal my brother! I won't let her touch him with her filthy—"

"Enough!" Nayaraq interrupted.

"But—"

Again Nayaraq interrupted him. "Leave. Now," she said to Ucho in a loud voice, pointing to the doorway.

Ucho glared at his mother. Then he turned his gaze on me. His eyes were narrow slits of spite, and his mouth was contorted in malice. "Don't touch him, Ugly One!" he warned as he backed out of the *wasi*.

"Don't listen to him," Nayaraq said. "Do what you have to do for my boy." Muti hadn't stopped his yelps and howls, and as we placed our hands on him and pressed him into the dirt floor, his cries grew even louder. He tried to twist this way and that, but my teacher and I both held him tightly as we chanted to the gods. The Paqo tucked the injured arm onto Muti's belly and bent it upward at the elbow. The boy's screams were so loud, I wanted to cover my ears, but I held him firmly. My teacher rotated the arm and shoulder outward as he pushed, trying to coax the shoulder back into place. We all felt the sudden *pop*. Almost immediately, Muti began to calm, and his crying quieted. The Paqo gently revolved the arm in the other direction, and we sang our thanks to the gods for allowing us to help the boy.

"Thank you," Nayaraq said to the Paqo. Then she turned to me. "Learning Girl, I apologize for my son's cruelty to you."

I wondered if she was aware of just how cruel her son had been to me all these years. Was she apologizing for today or for a lifetime of torment?

For now, I would have to be content knowing I had helped Muti. He was already sitting up on his own, and he was clearly uncomfortable being this close to me. Nayaraq carefully picked up her son and cradled him in her arms. I think Muti, Nayaraq, and I were *all* relieved when the two of them left the *wasi*. My teacher said nothing, just watched me watch them go with a bemused smile on his face.

One of my favorite visitors was Tica, a young wife who came to see the Paqo toward the end of her first pregnancy. She was swollen and bloated and uncomfortable. I placed my hands on her enormous belly, and she didn't flinch or move away from my touch at all.

"I think I'm too big. I have never seen another pregnant woman like this," she said. The Paqo and I nodded. It was true. Tica's middle was rounder than Mama Killa at her fullest.

"New Voice, why is she so large?" the Paqo asked.

I studied Tica with my hands and my heart, listening to the spirits around us and the new life growing inside her. Tica massaged her back, which was clearly paining her. The life within her moved. It was strong, but there was a strangeness to this movement that made me ask, "Are there two babies?"

The Paqo smiled. "I believe so."

Tica's eyes grew wide in surprise. "Two babies? Are they healthy?"

The spirits didn't speak to me of any troubles inside her, just the two heartbeats. "They seem to be," I said.

"No wonder I'm so big!" Tica laughed in relief as she rubbed her belly.

"We can give you medicine that will help with the swelling," I told her. "But I think it won't be long before the babies are ready to be born."

Tica left the *wasi* kissing her fingers and offering

both of us her thanks. The Paqo and I smiled at each other. The birth of one child was cause enough for celebration. Two babies was a bountiful gift from the gods.

The very next day I saw Tica carrying a new blanket through the center of the *llaqta*, waddling as she went. I offered to carry it for her, and she accepted with a look of gratitude. We walked slowly, Tica with both hands pressed firmly against her lower back, me admiring the blanket's intricately woven patterns of leaves and feathers.

"It's for the babies," she explained.

"It's beautiful," I told her. Sumac bobbed his head and squawked his bird agreement from my shoulder, causing Tica to laugh. Then he lowered his head carefully under her chin and held it there, something he had only ever done with me before.

"He is asking you to pet his head," I said in surprise.

Carefully, Tica raised her hand and petted him. "Like this?" she asked. Sumac moved his head to the other side, showing her his favorite spot.

"Yes. I think he likes you very much!"

The Handsome One grabbed a piece of Tica's hair in his beak and preened it slowly, carefully. "I think you're right," she replied with a pleased smile.

We chatted about the babies as we made our way

to Tica's home, and she thanked me as she took the blanket from me and went inside. I'm certain that this casual talk as we walked side by side through the village for all to see was a small thing for Tica, tinier than a pebble, but it meant so much more to me. I wondered if this was what it felt like to have a human friend.

13
UCHO
Hot Pepper

TWO moons passed before I realized that danger lurked in the shadows, licking its lips and waiting for the perfect moment to strike. I had thought Ucho was done tormenting me, but he came back with a surprising vengeance.

I was lying on the ground after my morning sun prayer, watching Sumac fly in the sky world. I had tried often to repeat my magical flight with him, and it is true I had joined the Handsome One many times as he soared through the air. But I wasn't certain it was the same. I think I was reliving the memory of the first time I had flown with him rather than joining him in spirit again. Every day, he stayed in the sky a little longer and flew a bit farther away. And each time he left, my heart beat more quickly, both in hope that this time I would join him right and true, and in fear that he would choose to stay with Inti forever rather than return to me.

On this morning, Sumac had flown far enough that I could no longer see him. I squinted against the bright rays of Inti and kept my eyes on the horizon, thinking the same words I always did when he flew too far away: *Come back to me.*

Suddenly, a large clump of dirt hit me in the face, exploding into many smaller pieces that filled my eyes and nose, making me cough and sputter. I stood quickly. Ucho's cruel laughter echoed slightly as he strode toward me. I rubbed the dirt from my face and ran my fingers through my hair to cover my scarred cheek. It was a gesture I had repeated countless times in the past, but ever since Sumac had chosen my right shoulder as his constant perch, I hadn't needed it. The thick black strands fell over my right eye, but I watched Ucho with my left as if he were a jaguar ready to pounce. At least he was alone.

"Finally, that feathered menace is gone long enough that I can do what I want!" Ucho snarled.

He pushed me roughly, but I stood stiff and tall. I would not let him knock me over. I would not let him see my fear.

"*You* might think we're finished, but we're not," Ucho went on. "I don't care that you fixed my brother's shoulder. There is no balance between us, Ugly One! My mother rambles on and on to me about you. I know I must be in your future, and I won't ignore my duty. But I warn you, I will make you miserable every day."

His scarred nose and hot breath were too close to my face. His anger pulsed its way through my skin and squeezed my heart. Why did he hate me so? Were these new threats because of what Sumac had done to his nose? Or did Ucho torment me because I was so ugly?

"And that evil shaman friend of yours? He won't be protecting you much longer!" Ucho continued with another shove. "There is already talk of sending him away. He is the reason the rains don't come. All the people are saying so. They will drive him out of the village forever, and they will kill your bird. Then I will come for you, Loathsome One!" He shook his head in disgust. "That hair doesn't hide anything. My scar is nothing compared with yours. You are hideous. Who would ever choose a life with you? I would poke out my eyes so I wouldn't have to gaze upon such a hideous wife."

A loud squawking from above suddenly gave me hope. I risked glancing upward, and true enough,

Sumac was flying toward us. I was filled with grati-tude, but taking my eyes from Ucho was a mistake. He seized the opportunity to push me off my feet. I landed on my side with such force, my breath rushed past my lips. As I lay on the earth, dust rising up in a thick haze, Sumac plummeted toward me with a loud cry. There was no confusing the sound he made. He would attack Ucho with his entire feathered being. Ucho realized this, for he scrambled off just before the Handsome One landed next to me.

I felt a pain above my eye, and when I put my hand to my forehead, it was wet and sticky. I pulled my fingers away and saw a small smear of blood, as red as Sumac's regal back. A sharp rock glistened next to me on the ground. I must have hit my head on it when I fell. Sumac bobbed his head in agitation. I reached out with my other hand and petted him, try-ing to soothe him as much as myself.

I considered telling someone about Ucho's attack. Ucho had often hurt me with his words, but never before with his hands. This wasn't the way of our people. But what if he blamed Sumac? What if it was decided that the bird was somehow at fault? I couldn't risk losing my feathered companion. He was so much more than a friend to me. He was my shield in life, my link to Beyond, my connection to my own self. I held him close to my face, breathing in his feathery belly, trying to reassure both of us.

As soon as I felt steady, I rose and made my way to the Paqo's *wasi*. He was the one person who could comfort me and bring stillness to my spirit. Thoughts spun about in my mind like a swirl of dust caught in the wind, but the ones that spiraled back the strongest were Ucho's words about the shaman. *He is the reason the rains don't come. They will drive him out of the village forever.*

回同

The Paqo and I sat outside his *wasi* by a small fire he had built. He had treated my forehead with a poultice of dried plant leaves mixed with water.

"It's a small scrape. There will be no scar," he said, but his voice was detached, and his eyes studied the faraway mountains, as if he were not truly with me.

"Thank you," I said. Then, to lighten the heaviness I felt, I added, "I didn't think I needed another one."

This brought a chuckle from my teacher. "Scars are interesting things, New Voice. Ucho will carry the one on his nose for the rest of his days."

"I think he must be very angry about that," I replied.

"Who would be happy to gain such a scar?"

I touched the river skin by my lip. Ucho's nose wasn't nearly as horrid to look upon as my disfigured face. Then again, he hadn't given me my scar, and I was partly responsible for his.

"He said he will make me miserable for the rest of my days."

"The boy speaks rashly. He lives up to his name, Hot Pepper." The Paqo sighed. He spoke slowly now, and each word seemed weighted with meaning. "Names are interesting things."

I studied my feet as I whispered, "Yes."

"Your sister, she calls you Micay."

"Yes. It's my birth name."

"Micay. Beautiful Round Face."

"I've been told I was a beautiful baby with a perfect, round face," I said. It was impossible for me to imagine this baby self. I had always been the Ugly One. Beautiful Round Face was some other person, some other baby, not me.

The Paqo said, "Strange how close the two names are. Micay. Millay. Beauty and horror just a click of the tongue apart. One moment in time, and a life veers off on a different path."

"Yes."

We sat in silence. The fire cracked and popped.

"Why do you sit on the rock?" he asked.

I didn't understand. My bottom rested flat upon the earth. But then, I never knew when an unexpected question might wind its way to me from the shaman. "I'm not sitting on a rock," I said cautiously, wary of a trick from my teacher.

"The rock you sit on so often. Why do you sit on that rock?"

He meant my *huaca*. Did he know it held a spirit? I wondered if he might take it from me if I told him, but to lie to the shaman wasn't possible. "It holds power. It is a *huaca*."

The Paqo waved his hand dismissively at what I had thought was an important revelation. "Of course it is a *huaca*. But there are many *huaca*. What drew you to that one?"

I had never wondered this before. "I'm not certain. I think it must have called to me."

"It's good that you have it. You will need its strength," the shaman said, and then his gaze fixed itself once again upon some faraway point. His eyes became distant, like secrets carved in stone.

I wanted to ask if I would need the strength of the *huaca* because the Paqo would be leaving soon. Were the people going to drive him away? Did he know this already? And I wondered, if he had truly been a mighty shaman in the capital city of Cuzco, why had he left there to come to our small, unimportant *llaqta*? Had he done something terrible? I needed him here with me. What would I do if he left? These questions lurked in my throat, but I remained quiet as I sat next to my teacher. As long as I didn't ask them, I didn't have to act on the answers.

⊡⊡

It was as I sat on my rush mat, eating the meager evening meal with my family, that I gathered the courage to place my questions into the air for others to hear. "I've been told that the people blame the Paqo for the lack of rains," I said, forcing my voice to be clear and steady. "I've heard they want to drive him out of the village. Is this true?"

Mama, Papa, and Chasca went still, their spoons frozen in midair. Only the steam from the *quwi* stew continued to move lazily upward, as if nothing unusual had just happened. Without them saying a word, I knew it was true. Ucho had been right.

The silence became awkward. Father cleared his throat, and I could see he was about to rattle off some nonsense. Chasca leaned toward me and spoke first. She put her hand softly on mine and smiled faintly.

"Don't worry, Micay. They are too scared of the shaman to actually do it."

I nodded at my sister, and my family continued with the meal, trying to pretend all was well when it was not. I wondered, *How long will it be before the people's fear of hunger overpowers their fear of my teacher?*

14

CAPAC RAYMI

Magnificent Festival

THREE worlds dwell within the night sky," the Paqo said as he pointed toward the stars flickering their small, icy fires. We were lying on the ground studying the countless twinkling daughters of Inti and Mama Killa on this most important of nights, Capac Raymi. It was the shortest night of the year, the only night when, for one breathless moment at dawn, the barriers between this world and the spirit world were bridged.

"There is the below world, the land of the past and our ancestors, home of the ground-dwelling fox, the toad, and the mighty serpent." The Paqo pointed low in the black cloth of the night sky, and there, in the pattern of the stars, were the ground animals. He continued. "Just above is this world, the place of now, the dwelling of the plants, the people, and the fierce jaguar." Here he pointed to midsky and the stars outlining the jaguar ready to pounce. "And higher yet is the upper world, the future, home of the sky spirits, the rainbow, lightning, stars, sun, moon, and condor." He pointed to the stars in the uppermost sky, drawing the shape of the condor in flight with his fingers.

The Paqo sat up, and I did the same. "Each animal has its own message, its own meaning," he said. "The serpent below, the jaguar in the middle, and the condor above, one sitting atop the other. And all three worlds are connected through the spiral." With his finger, he made a rising spiral in the night air. His voice was quiet and solemn as he asked, "But what else is there, New Voice, aside from the spiral, aside from these worlds?"

Like most people, I knew of the three worlds and the spiral connecting them. But I had not heard of anything else. "There is more?" I asked in surprise.

The Paqo chuckled. "New Voice, where is it you seek to be?"

I sought to be where I was, studying the stars with my teacher. There was nowhere I would rather be, but I thought I knew what his question meant. "Beyond?"

He grunted in approval. "*Ari*. Beyond. The hummingbird represents Beyond."

I had never truly thought about what Beyond actually was or where it could be found. Was it a place?

Did hummingbirds flitter their way to the stars? Was Beyond past the stars?

Difficult questions often churned within me when I was with the Paqo, but even so I treasured our time together. I would rather be confused sitting under the stars with him than be with the people, as we had been earlier that night. Ordinarily, I would have enjoyed the festival of Capac Raymi, when the conch shell was blown loudly to the sky to welcome the spirit world on this shortest of nights. But I preferred to forget this night's celebration. Not because the conch call had felt weak, as if it couldn't even reach to the tops of the mountains, let alone carry our message all the way to the sky world. And not because the feast had been so meager that the people could barely smile at one another. I chose to forget this night because of the disturbing glances cast toward my teacher when the people thought he wasn't looking.

I had been oblivious to these glances before, but once Ucho opened my eyes, I saw how some people felt. They blamed the Paqo for the hard times. They murmured that if he were a good shaman right and true, the spirits wouldn't be punishing us. They asked in accusing whispers, *Didn't the rains slow the very year he arrived in the village?* Fear flickered on their faces like a hungry, growing flame. I am willing to say I was glad they were scared, for it prevented them from taking action. But it was just a matter of time before the pain of empty stomachs swallowed their fear of my teacher. And then he would be gone.

"The llama leads the sky river to our world," the Paqo went on, and I was glad for this moment, this now. The llama in the sky was formed in the blackness between the stars. I knew the boys who tended the llama herd would be performing their own special ceremonies and customs in the days that followed to ensure the safety and fortune of our village's animals.

We sat together now, the Paqo and I, watching. I tried to spy any stars coming down to the earth as shimmering, golden-haired maidens. There certainly wasn't any corn for them to steal. The mighty sky river lowered breath by breath, its sacred light following a path it had known since before the time of the ancestors. Finally, just before the dawn, it hovered on the horizon and touched the land. Earth world and spirit world were one.

The Paqo rose and began to chant. I stood by his side, staring at the connected worlds. My entire body tingled, especially my shoulder where Sumac's claws dug tightly into the skin. My teacher's voice swirled around me and rose into the endless above. With each hushed breath I took, the cold air wrapped itself around my beating heart and lifted the hairs on my neck. I felt the connection of all the worlds and the endless power of the spiral. It wasn't Beyond, but I was filled with gratitude for this moment.

The Paqo finished his chant and turned to me. "New Voice, it is time to tell you. I will be leaving."

So it was true. My teacher would abandon me. Next, the people would take Sumac away. I would be alone, and it would be worse than ever before, for now I knew what it meant to have constant companionship, both human and feathered. How could I bear to return to my old way of being?

I was trying to be brave, and the effect of my fears combined with bent courage must have given me a comical appearance, for suddenly the shaman laughed mightily, the gap in his front teeth showing in the moonlight. He put his fingers on my shoulder, and Sumac moved closer to my face to make room for the strong hand. "Don't despair. I'm going on a journey. I won't be gone long."

I could feel my entire body shaking like a tender leaf in a powerful gust of wind, my relief was so great.

"I must go to meet with the other shamans. It is time to find out what we have done to displease the spirits. The *paqos* must join powers to talk with the other world."

I heard this explanation, but my mind was focused inward. I was repeating, *It is a short journey. He isn't leaving forever. He isn't leaving me.* But the Paqo's next words brought me back. "And you will come with me, New Voice."

Again I offered an expression that my teacher found humorous.

"Don't look so surprised. How else are you to learn the ways of the shaman?"

He felt I was worthy! The mighty Paqo wanted me to accompany him on an important journey as his apprentice. I tried to tell him I would follow this path and make him proud, but no words could find their way past the lump that suddenly lodged in my throat like a huge boulder. I tried to stand tall and look at him with eyes that could stare down challenges and not falter, but my shoulders shook and my eyes filled with tears. Still, I kept my gaze firmly on my teacher, and his eyes held mine securely, like a strong tree trunk one could clutch in a storm. He smiled as the tears trickled their way down my cheeks.

I lifted my fingers to my lips and kissed the tips in reverence. *"Pachis,"* I said in a shaky whisper, glad to have the word sound at all.

My teacher nodded and spoke in a voice I had never heard before, matching my quiet tone. "Don't thank me yet, New Voice. On a journey such as this, one can never know what might happen. The spirits are already angry for reasons no one understands." He paused, then added with a hint of fear in his voice, "I can only hope they will be kind to us."

I wasn't certain if the Paqo meant the spirits or the other shamans. I realized that I still didn't know the right and true reasons why the Paqo had come to our *llaqta*. If the wagging tongues of the people were correct, he had been exiled to our small place in the mountains by the Sapa Inca himself. How would such a shaman be received by the other *paqos*? And what would they think of the Ugly One trailing along behind him?

15
TASKIKARU
Journey

ARE you certain you have enough blankets to keep you warm?" Mama questioned as I put the last of my things into a wrap to carry on my back. The nights would be cold, though we would have the protective walls of the *tampus*, the guesthouses set along the trail for travelers.

"Yes, Mama," I said. "I packed the warmest ones you made for me." I hoped my calm voice would reassure her. I knew it wasn't easy for her to watch me go. I remembered back almost three years ago when Hatun left to work for the Sapa Inca, guarding and repairing the many roads that wove their way to the four corners of the empire. Hatun had been eager to serve his time, as all boys did when they became young men. He had been impatient with Mama as she fussed over him in the moments before he left. I vowed not to snap at her as he had done.

Mama's face creased with lines of worry. She asked, "You will be careful?"

"Yes, Mama."

"You will mind the Paqo? Listen to what he says?"

"Yes, Mama."

"Do not leave his side."

"I won't, Mama."

"And you will come back to us?" I could tell that this last question was the one that truly mattered. Mama didn't want to lose her youngest child. I knew she was being brave, trying to say goodbye with grace, but it was difficult for her.

I placed my hands on her shoulders as I answered. "Of course, Mama. I will come back to you."

"Wife, let the child be," said Father. "She is under the protection of the mighty Paqo. She will be fine." Father's faith in the shaman was complete. As far as he was concerned, Mama's distress was bothersome. He would rather spend his time worrying about more important things, such as the number of owl hoots he'd heard in the night or how many spiders he'd sighted scurrying across his path.

Chasca pulled Mama toward her. "Micay will be

fine. Don't be scared," she said, and Mama let Chasca hug her tightly in reassurance.

As I left our *wasi* and walked to the Paqo's home with Sumac perched proudly on my shoulder, I thought about how Mama hadn't leaned in to kiss me goodbye. I would have turned away as I always did to save her from having to kiss such an ugly daughter, but I was sad that she hadn't even tried.

回厄

I had heard much of the great Incan trails that crisscrossed our mighty empire. I knew my brother and other young men devoted years to maintaining the roads and their little sisters, the bridges. But I had never journeyed along these paths before. I hadn't shown my fear to Mama, but of course I was nervous to leave my home.

The Gathering was to take place at Wiñay Wayna, a holy place several days away that was known for its beautiful orchids and many flowing fountains. Wiñay Wayna was not far from Sacred Sun City at Machu Picchu. I would be close to the Sacred Rock that spoke its powerful messages to those who were worthy, a rock whose presence I felt more and more strongly as we made our way on the path. But we weren't going to Sacred Sun City.

"New Voice, these travel days will be a good time for

you to learn new lessons," the Paqo said as we walked. He wore two golden-yellow feathers in his hair holder so others would recognize him for the powerful shaman he was. His feet set a fast pace, and I hurried to remain with him. Sumac dug his claws in deeply so he wouldn't fall off my shoulder. He was quietly squawking a tune Mama liked to hum while she prepared the evening meal.

"Yes, Paqo," I said. A lesson from my teacher sounded exactly right. It would distract me from the newness of my surroundings and put me at ease.

"You must study what you see around you. That is your lesson during our journey."

I laughed quietly at these words. The Paqo wouldn't distract me from my unease; he would place it in front of me for inspection.

He continued. "You will learn to speak with the world, New Voice."

"I will learn to speak with the world," I said dutifully.

It was his turn to chuckle. "I know this trick of yours. You mimic my words when you have no new ones. You don't understand me."

"No."

"There is the language of the people, the human tongue, and there is also the language of the world.

Here is the lesson: Let us speak to the world about the rain. What here tells you about rain?"

I studied the surroundings. A small rock shrine sat on the left side of the road. Travelers had placed little stones, twisted straw, and dried flowers at its base to ensure a safe journey. The only signs of green were the pale patches of lichen strangling the living rocks on which they grew. It was dry everywhere. So dry. We kicked up dust from the road with each step, and it tickled and clung to the inside of my nose.

"There is little water. There is much dust."

"True, but there is more to observe, and there is less to observe."

I remained quiet, trying to decipher what the Paqo meant now. I studied my feet as I walked, heel touching the earth, then the toe. Heel, toe, dust; heel, toe, dust. Less to observe?

"What is missing here, New Voice?"

"Water. Plants."

"Yes. The earth cries out to us with her dust. She speaks of her thirst through the dust. There are no *maca-maca* plants sprouting upward. This path should be filled with heart-shaped hoof prints from the deer, but no. No *maca-maca*, no deer. If the plants die, we die. All are one."

It was easy to see the earth was thirsty, but could we listen to her well enough to know if it would rain? Could we make it rain?

"Will the rains come?" I asked.

"That is the purpose of the Gathering. But it will not rain today." The Paqo pointed to some thin clouds that tore themselves upon the jagged-crested mountains in the distance. "Those clouds don't speak of rain. They will dry up before they can shed a drop."

It was at this point that we saw our first fellow traveler. I knew immediately he was a *chasqui*, a foot messenger, one of the men who ran along the roads delivering news and goods to the four corners of the empire. I had never seen one before, but I had heard of them, and it was easy to sight him with his sunbonnet covered in white feathers and his shell horn. He slowed as he neared us. Reverently, he placed the tips of his fingers to his mouth and kissed them in honor of the Paqo.

"Mighty Paqo, it is good to see you."

The Paqo nodded his head in acknowledgment. "Are you on the fish route?"

"Yes. I have just handed it off to the next runner."

The Paqo explained to me, "The runners deliver fish from the ocean all the way to the capital city. The emperor enjoys eating freshly caught fish at least once a day."

There was a pause, then the *chasqui* said awkwardly, "Mighty Paqo, might I ask something of you?"

"Of course."

"Could you read the leaves for me? I would like to know some things that will come to pass in my future."

The Paqo nodded and removed his *koka* pouch from his side. It was made of brown *vicuña* wool, a luxury reserved for the highest of noblemen and shamans. Carefully, he extracted a handful of dried leaves from within. The messenger cupped his hands, and the shaman placed the green pile inside the eagerly outstretched palms.

"New Voice, step away," the Paqo said quietly. "This is a private task."

I watched from a short distance as the shaman studied the *koka* plant intently, examining the leaf patterns and listening to their inner wisdom. The *chasqui* remained very still, very silent, so as not to interrupt the Paqo's concentration. Finally, I saw the Paqo's lips moving, telling of what he saw in the runner's future. Both faces were grave, and when the Paqo was done, the messenger's expression was fearful. I waited until he had said his thank-you and goodbye before approaching my teacher again.

"His face spoke, Paqo. It spoke of bad news."

The Paqo watched the *chasqui*'s figure as it grew smaller along the path. Soon it disappeared altogether around the nearest bend.

"I cannot share another's future with you."

"I wasn't asking."

"You wouldn't object if I told you."

I admit I was curious to know what the Paqo had said to make the poor messenger so fearful. "True."

"It can be a dangerous thing, to learn of your future." My teacher turned to me with sad eyes. "Would you ask me to read the *koka* leaves for you, New Voice?"

It had never occurred to me to request this of my teacher. I didn't feel prepared, especially to receive bad news as the runner had. "Not today, Paqo."

My teacher nodded his head in approval. "Good, New Voice." His face clearly spoke to me as he said this. It spoke of relief.

回回

There isn't much to tell of the next few days as we made our way to the shaman gathering. We set a brisk pace, walking what felt to be great distances away from home, slowing only when the path became steeper. At night, we slept in the guesthouses. The Sapa Inca's men collected food from the villages every season and placed it in the many storehouses for travelers and for the people to eat in the years when the crops didn't grow. The Paqo told me that these guesthouses were normally stocked with corn, potatoes, and dried strips of llama meat, as well as wood for fire. All the storehouses we encountered were empty now except of firewood. It was good that we had brought our own food, but I feared that without rainfall the storerooms would remain empty and the people would wither and die like the kernels they had planted in the ground.

Each night our presence was recorded on the *quipus,* colored strings tied to a long branch of wood. The *quipu* recorders placed intricate knots in the strings to indicate our ages and our purpose for traveling. They also noted the supplies we used from the storehouses so they could be properly restocked, though we used only the firewood. I wondered what they thought of Sumac, riding as always on my shoulder, but no one questioned his presence.

On the last day, we began descending. I saw mosses and fruit trees and crop fields filled with peanuts, chili peppers, and *koka* leaves. The cloud forest air was rich and thick to my lungs, which were used to higher, thinner air. I inhaled its green, living scent. It was on this day that I first spoke right and true with the world.

The Paqo was again speaking of the importance of

listening and watching properly. "The more you observe, New Voice, the more you understand. Once you can interpret the voice of the world, you become its revealer. Birds are strong messengers of the world."

I agreed. "Sumac has been an excellent messenger. He brought me to you." I reached up and stroked the bird slowly on his belly and under his wing. This was a favored spot. He leaned his head into my cheek for support and lifted the wing higher, letting out small squeaking sounds of contentment.

"Yes, but let us discuss other birds. The condor. The hummingbird. They are opposites, no? They balance each other." The Paqo spread his arms wide like condor wings. "The condor is big, slow. It lives on the flesh of the dead and transports the dead to Beyond." He brought his arms close to his sides and fluttered them quickly. "The hummingbird is small, fast. It lives on flowers."

As if he had called it to us, a small hummingbird suddenly flitted past, hovering in the air in front of us before swerving off to the left.

The Paqo beamed. "A message for us!" He stopped walking and asked, "New Voice, what did the hummingbird reveal?"

I pulled my hand back from Sumac to scratch my

head in confusion. The Handsome One squawked in protest, then fluffed himself out and began preening his belly feathers as if to show he didn't need my assistance.

I wondered, had the hummingbird come from Beyond? And if not, where had it come from? We hadn't seen other such birds on the journey.

"Aha!" I yelled loudly enough to surprise both the Paqo and Sumac.

"Yes?" the shaman urged.

I stood tall as I spoke, for I knew I had figured out the answer to this world riddle. "The hummingbird told us that our journey has almost ended. We are near to Wiñay Wayna."

"How do you know this to be so?" the Paqo asked with a serious face, but I could see he was pleased.

"Hummingbirds live on flowers. Birds and flowers, they are as one. Orchids and other flowers grow at Wiñay Wayna. It is named for them. The hummingbird must be near its home. It came to greet us."

The smile my teacher offered shone almost as brightly upon me as the golden rays of Inti. I basked in the warmth.

"You have spoken well with the world today, New Voice. We have been welcomed to Wiñay Wayna. Our journey is over. We have arrived at the Gathering."

16
WIÑAY WAYNA
Forever Young

IT is difficult to tell you right and true how I felt walking down the stone steps to Wiñay Wayna. Imagine a pool of water, a large puddle perhaps. See this puddle in your mind. Bring it into being. Now imagine a rock thrown into its center. The water moves, splashes for a moment. Now see many rocks being thrown into the puddle. Water ripples and splashes everywhere. The dirt from beneath is stirred up and browns the water. Rock after rock is thrown into the puddle, and mud and water churn. My stomach was this puddle. The rocks were the many questions and fears within me. Would I be shunned by the other shamans? What was their true opinion of my teacher? What would the Gathering be like? Would we be able to speak with the gods? Would it rain? These rock questions piled up inside me, but

I tried to keep a calm outside as the Paqo, Sumac, and I made our way toward a group of five shamans standing near one of the small trickling fountains.

They turned as one to face us when we neared. Four of them were shaman priests, the last a priestess. All wore the traditional dual golden feathers, the color of the sweat of the sun. The lines in their faces spoke of many years of healing and listening to the people and the world. Their eyes were deep lakes filled with old wisdom. The woman's hair flowed long and silver, and she held a beautifully carved wooden staff for support. All placed their fingers to their lips. The Paqo and I also kissed our fingers, and I bowed deeply.

"Welcome," the woman said with a smile filled with confidence and grace.

One of the men was somewhat younger than the others and more elaborately decorated. Large plugs of pure gold shone in his pierced earlobes. A necklace of jaguar teeth and carved seashells hung heavily upon his chest. There was strength in his high cheekbones and curved nose as well as in the way he held himself. But it was the manner in which the other four stepped subtly aside as he approached the Paqo that told of his supreme authority. I chose to move a pace away, unsure where to be but knowing that by my teacher's side was not the right place.

The Paqo and this man stood nose to nose, inter-locking gazes with an intensity that caused me to avert my eyes. Even so, I could feel the air between them expanding and crackling, as if the lightning god himself were about to strike the earth.

The Paqo spoke first. "Villac Uma, it is good to see you."

This man was the Villac Uma, the head priest and highest sorcerer of the entire empire? He rivaled the emperor himself in power! The holiest of temples were his to command, as well as the Sun Maidens and all other shaman priests. At his word, a hundred llamas would be sacrificed, the emperor would fast for ten days, a statue of pure gold would be erected in honor of any of the deities. The very flow of the rivers was determined by this man and the gods he called his equals.

The Villac Uma nodded slowly. "Yes. It is good to see you as well, old friend." His voice was like low thunder, deep and rumbling with strength. "I see you have brought your apprentice."

All eyes turned to me. Was this a time to speak or to remain silent? To bow my head or jut out my chin in false confidence? Sumac bobbed his head at the shamans and comfortably puffed his feathers. I wished I had his ease of spirit. I wanted to bury my face behind his solid body.

"Yes," the Paqo replied. He spoke with an air of firmness, as if to prove a point. "It is right and true for her to be here."

The others exchanged quiet looks. It was as I feared. My presence at the Gathering was causing a problem.

The Villac Uma and the Paqo began speaking without words. The head priest posed a question. I could see it in his raised eyebrows. The Paqo replied in a manner that clearly pleased the Villac Uma. Both men suddenly smiled.

The head priest announced for all to hear, "Welcome, Yachachisqa, Apprentice Girl. It is good that you are here."

Slowly, I made my way to the Villac Uma and dropped to my knees. "*Pachis*. I am honored."

Before I had the chance to bask in his acceptance, the Villac Uma spoke again to the Paqo. "The people are growing hungrier every day. The Sapa Inca is asking if it is time for a human sacrifice to appease the gods. We will ask the spirits tonight."

The Paqo nodded in agreement.

The priestess spoke in a voice like a clear moving stream, "Inti moves across the sky. We must prepare for the night's ceremonies."

"The last four will be here soon," the Villac Uma said. Then he turned to the Paqo. "No one has claimed your favored spot, old friend. Settle in. We will see you at moonrise."

The Paqo nodded his agreement, and the five shamans moved away so quickly and quietly as to leave me wondering if they had been there at all.

Without a word I stood, and the Paqo and I made our way into the heart of Wiñay Wayna to prepare ourselves.

🔲🔲

Feelings that are true sink deep into the heart, where they remain. The ceremony that evening would not go well. No one had told me, but I knew this to be so. I felt it in every beat of my heart.

I knew the ceremony wouldn't go well as the Paqo and I laid out our rush mats in his favored spot, one of the many small stone guesthouses covered with thatch. Outside, the creamy petals of orchids reflected the pale glow of twilight, and a friendly fountain gurgled. It was strange and pleasant to hear water. The Paqo explained that the orchids were fewer and many of the fountains had slowed or dried up altogether because of the drought. He was glad this one was still running. He hung his hummingbird weaving in the open doorway. We would only stay the one night, but it was important to give this place a sense of home and familiarity.

I knew the ceremony wouldn't go well as we walked

through Wiñay Wayna to the Gathering. There were few people living their days and nights there. It was primarily a storage center for crops collected throughout the empire. It was also a holy place for washing and preparing, a last stop before reaching Sacred Sun City at Machu Picchu. The absence of other people added a strange sense of stillness.

I knew the ceremony wouldn't go well as the Paqo left me seated on a large boulder near several of the other shamans and walked up to join the Villac Uma in the center of the activities. I was feeling the mood of the world. The rains would not come, and the powerful shaman priests and priestesses seemed to know this even as they prepared themselves that evening. The spirits would deliver us the message of no rain right and true. Watch and you will see how they did so.

One of the shamans was the firekeeper. He stood by a mighty blaze that popped and crackled, telling him when to add more wood, where to place dried lichen, and how to keep the fire from growing too enormous to control. The blaze was bigger than any I had ever seen. It flared upward like a stream of hot orange waves trying to course their way to the sky world. I don't know how the keeper stayed as close to the flames as he did, for the heat was almost unbearable from where I was sitting, but he watched and listened to the fire with his entire being, and the blaze responded to his every movement as if they were one.

This ceremony tonight was in honor of Illapa, god of thunder and lightning. His body was made of stars, and he wore a cloak sewn from pure lightning. Illapa ruled in the sky with a club in one hand and a sling in the other. His sister sat nearby cradling a jug of water. When he chose to, Illapa would sling a stone at his sister's jug. The shattering of the jug created thunder, and the water pouring forth was the rain. As the servant and messenger of Inti, Illapa was the proper god with whom to speak this night.

"O Great Illapa, Flashing One, hear us!" the Villac Uma boomed suddenly.

All became silent at the Villac Uma's words, all except the fire, which crackled and spat more violently. My teacher slipped away from the head priest's side and returned holding a long rope. Attached to the other end was a llama. The animal was blacker than the fiercest of rain clouds. It would be our messenger to the spirit world.

As the Villac Uma took a *tumi,* a ceremonial knife, from his pouch, I noticed that the sacrifice of a llama was different without an audience to impress. Movements were made without flourish, and the ten shaman priests and priestesses focused more on one another and the quiet world of the inside than on the outside appearance of the ceremony. I was witnessing a moment of true power and communication with Beyond.

With sure motions, the Villac Uma removed the heart of the black llama and held it up for all to see. Here was the first bad omen. The heart stopped beating immediately, a clear sign that the path would continue to be difficult.

The Paqo held up a silver goblet that shone in the clear light of the moon. He poured some *aca* into the goblet and handed it to the Villac Uma. The two men concentrated on the heart of the llama, and all the gathered shamans also studied the heart intently, speaking to it in praise and trying to listen to its message. The Villac Uma squeezed the heart over the goblet, and the blood dripped into the silver container.

I was glad now for the heat of the fire, as the night air was cold enough to show my breath. I saw the words of the shamans hang in the frigid air as they chanted the traditional prayer together. "O fountain of water which for so many years has watered the fields, through which blessings we gather our food, do the same this year. Pour down the waters, and give if it pleases even more water, so that the harvest this year may be in abundance."

At the completion of the prayer, the Villac Uma made ready to pour the contents of the silver goblet into a still pool of water resting within a flat oval stone. The action of the water was critical. If the blood and *aca* mixture fell easily into the pool and was accepted like a good rain soaking into the earth, this would be a powerful sign that rains would come and quench Earth Mother's thirst.

With all the shamans focused on him, the Villac Uma tipped the goblet slowly and carefully. But the liquid from within bounced on the still water like a violent rainstorm that erodes the land. This was enough to confirm that the time of the drought would continue. However, one more message was sent to us at this time.

A sudden shout from the firekeeper drew everyone's attention. Somehow, perhaps in his watching the Villac Uma, the keeper had stopped listening to his fire for a moment. A flame had taken hold of his cloak and set it on fire. With a screech, he dropped to the ground and began rolling in the dust. He quickly put the fire out in this manner and stood, looking bewildered by what had just happened.

A dead heart. Violent waters. A hungry fire that tried to eat its keeper. Can you see how clearly the spirits spoke with us?

The Villac Uma waved his hands at the gathered shamans. "It is time to go," he said. "No rains will come. Fast for the next two moon cycles. Speak with the spirits and ask for guidance. We will appease the gods with a human sacrifice."

I had known the ceremony wouldn't go well, but I didn't know what the people would do, now that it was certain there would be no rains.

17
CURACAS
Inspectors

TWO moon cycles passed. My teacher fasted throughout this time, and my lessons were fewer as he spent many of his days and nights alone speaking with the spirits. I didn't fast, although food was scarce enough that hunger hung in my belly much of the time. The grains in our village's storehouses were almost gone, and everyone was careful not to take too much.

The first member of our *llaqta* died from the hard times. It was old Sutic. I checked on Cora often after he died. Her sadness was so heavy, it took away her voice. I sat with her for a while every day in silence and simply held her hand. Smoke from the burning *muña* plant filled the *wasi* during these quiet moments. I wasn't sure if her headaches still came, but she seemed to like the smell, so I brought some with me every visit. Sometimes Sumac's silly head bobs and unhappy Father sighs would bring a small smile to her lips, but that was all.

We heard that a young Sun Maiden, only ten years old, was sacrificed. The Villac Uma selected her from among the many beautiful girls in the Acllahuasi in the capital city of Cuzco. She was sacrificed from atop a mighty mountain, the highest place a human could reach, in the hopes that her pure and beautiful spirit would speak to Inti on behalf of the people. She had come from a village not too far from our own. How I envied this chosen girl. I prayed that she spoke well to Inti, but so far no rains had come.

Planting season would begin again in two moons' time, and the people now turned their prayers to the next year's harvest. At least they hadn't tried to drive my teacher from the *llaqta*. He remained alone with his prayers, and they let him be. Instead, they came to me with their aches and pains and troubles. I did what I could to help, but most of them were simply starving, and I had no food for them. They looked at me with their tired, hungry eyes, and I asked the spirits to ease their suffering, to please help them. I especially didn't like to see the young ones this way. The hunger ate away their smiles and silenced their childish laughter.

No flowers grew from the dry and thirsty earth, but

Chasca bloomed so beautifully that the people couldn't help but stare when she walked by. She was almost sixteen and would marry in two years. My sister would have her pick of men, and she watched them all to see who pleased her the most. Then, lying in the *wasi* each evening, she would review her choices. "Hualpa has a nice face, but he never speaks with me. He is shyer than a deer. Cachi is not as handsome, but his eyes smile when he looks at me," she would explain. "And Titu brought me some dried *punga-punga* flowers. He said he wanted to bring me fresh flowers but there are simply none to be found."

"Any of them would be lucky to marry you. You are very pretty," I would whisper back, and my sister would bat her eyelashes and laugh.

Never did we discuss what might happen to me when *I* came of age. What was there to say? As Ucho had pointed out so often, who would want to marry the Loathsome One? At least my sister didn't insult me with false reassurances. It was easier for us to ignore the topic altogether.

The time of the annual inspections arrived. The emperor sent *curacas*, special men to take a census of the number of births and deaths and marriages that had taken place during the year. These inspectors also collected one-third of the crops, to be dried and placed in the storehouses for difficult times. It didn't take a mighty shaman to know that one-third of nothing was nothing. This year would be a sad time for inspections, right and true. Not that it was normally a joyful experience. When it came time to line up and answer the many questions posed by the emperor's nosy men, the saying among the people was "Keep quiet and you will not get into trouble."

The cool pulse of dawn was beginning to give way to the beating heat of midmorning when the two *curacas* arrived, as expected. The people gathered in the center of the village. Old Sutic would have been moved officially into the category of the elderly this inspection year, excusing him from the demanding physical tasks he so loathed. Instead, Cora stood alone, barely whispering that her husband had recently died when the inspectors reached her and poked her with their questions. The two men recorded this information on the official *quipu* strings. Next they recorded the birth of Tica's two children, a boy and a girl. She held them proudly as she announced their names to the *curacas*. Then the men continued through the people, asking questions and frowning.

"They are having a difficult year," Mama whispered to us. "All these villages to inspect, and no crops to collect."

Father shifted from foot to foot as he hissed, "Shhh! They are approaching. Do not speak. Do not look them in the eye! Avoid trouble!"

Chasca and I glanced at each other and smiled at Father's worry. We had nothing to hide, nothing of which to be frightened.

"Have there been any births or deaths in this family this year?" the taller of the two asked.

Father continued to stare at the dusty ground as he replied, "No."

"Your ages?"

As Father answered, the shorter man examined us, stepping in front of each of us one by one. Sumac had taken off in flight earlier and hadn't yet returned. It was for the best. No need to explain about the bird from the faraway *yunka* that lived with our family. The man's probing eyes searched me bottom to top, and I detected disgust as he sighted my scar. Quickly, he moved in front of Chasca. She kept her chin tucked coyly downward, sending her hair into a beautiful cascade of shimmering black, but her eyes peeked up at him. Now the man's sneer became a smile, and he raised his eyebrows slightly before he and his partner moved on to the next family. We were free to leave.

"Chasca! I told you to keep your eyes down! Oh, the

maggot of fire is dragging me toward the grave!" Father scolded as we made our way back to the *wasi*.

"Father, I tried," Chasca said. "Did you see the way he looked at me? It would have made trouble *not* to meet his gaze!"

"There is no use in worrying," Mama said in her calm way. "What has happened has happened."

After the *curacas* met with all the families, Yawar, our leader, led them through the village to examine the cleanliness of the homes and paths. He took them to the fields to confirm that nothing had grown. It was also Yawar's duty to communicate to the people any important decisions the inspectors had made. I recalled when Yawar had visited our family to say that it was time for Hatun to serve the emperor by helping with the roads and bridges. Tonight we expected a similar visit to tell us Hatun had finished his term of duty and would return home soon.

We had just finished the evening meal when we heard Yawar calling hello from outside our *wasi*.

"Yawar," Mama said. "Please, come in." She hastily cleared the floor and put down an extra rush mat for him to sit upon.

"I won't stay long," he said. "I have several other homes to visit."

Father and Mama nodded in understanding.

"Hatun will return as planned. He has served the emperor well and received much praise for his skill and dedication."

We all smiled. Father rose slightly, as if to end the visit, but Yawar placed a hand on his shoulder. "Eager for me to be done, eh?" he said. "But there is one more message from the inspectors for your family." He seemed aware that this announcement made us suddenly nervous, for he quickly added, "Don't be fearful. It is good."

Father sat, wringing his hands. He was unable to remain quiet. "What is the news? We weren't expecting any other changes this year! What do they want of us? How could it be good?"

Yawar chuckled. "It *is* good, right and true." He paused for dramatic effect. Uncle Turu, in the height of a good story, couldn't have done better himself, and we all leaned in closer. "Your daughter has been chosen to be a Sun Maiden. She will be a member of the Acllahuasi, the convent of the Sun Maidens!"

For the briefest, most foolish of moments, I thought that perhaps it was *I* who had been selected, but of course it was Chasca to whom Yawar now turned. "No one from our village has ever been chosen. You have honored us all."

Chasca had no choice in this matter. She couldn't refuse her selection, but why would she want to? She began to jump up and down like a happy frog. Father hooted with laughter and puffed out his chest with pride. I stood and hugged my sister with genuine happiness. I was jealous, true, but this wasn't a new emotion when it came to my feelings for my sister. Mama had tears in her eyes. She was proud of Chasca, but I could see that the tears were those of a mother who had just learned she would be saying goodbye to her elder daughter very soon.

Yawar continued, "Of course, Chasca is too old to be selected as a sacrifice. She will be married to a nobleman when she is eighteen, or perhaps she will be assigned to tend to the mummies."

The bodies of the past emperors were guarded carefully and brought out on special occasions. These mummies held strong powers and required constant attention from designated Sun Maidens. I smiled. There was no question which of these two fates my sister would prefer.

But Yawar wasn't done. "*And* she is to be sent to the Acllahuasi in Sacred Sun City, not the one in Cuzco," he added triumphantly.

This final revelation pierced my heart more painfully than the cruelest words Ucho had ever snarled at me. The Acllahuasi in the capital city was where most of the Sun Maidens dwelled. Why was she being sent to the convent in Sacred Sun City? The gods must truly despise me to send my sister to the place I most longed to be.

⊡⊡

I had feared that my teacher would leave me, but it had never occurred to me that I would be saying good-bye to my sister. We had only a small amount of time left together. When the moon waned and was almost eaten by the serpent in the sky, a *chasqui* runner would be sent to take her to Sacred Sun City to live with the other Sun Maidens. Chasca and I spent much of this time talking and sharing secrets, knowing that this would be our last chance to be sisters. We would most likely never see each other after she left.

The morning Chasca was to depart, we sat on my *huaca* eating dried potatoes. I had never shared my special place with anyone. Not even the Paqo had sat on my spirit rock with me. But it felt right and true to be there with my sister that day. "I hope I am given to a handsome nobleman," Chasca confided. "What if I am selected instead to be a Sun Maiden who tends to the mummies?"

"All the noblemen will want to marry you," I said with certainty.

"The Sun Maidens are all beautiful. Everyone knows this is so. It is not assured that I can catch an eye any more than another Maiden."

It was difficult to imagine an entire convent of women as lovely as Chasca, but her words were right and true. My sister's chances of marriage were suddenly uncertain, although not as uncertain as mine.

"What of you, Micay?" she asked, and I realized that as she was the only one who still called me Micay, when she left, my name of Beautiful Round Face truly would be a thing of the past.

I had wondered if Chasca might bring up this topic that we had so carefully avoided for so long. My future was unknown to me. Images of my possible paths darted through my mind like moths flitting about a fire. These moth ideas were difficult to fix in my head, and the flames devoured them before I could focus on any one long enough to see it clearly. There had been one possibility that had allowed me some hope: that I might become a shaman priestess. True, the people were coming to me with their troubles, but I required much more training. I had barely seen my teacher over the past two moons, and the people were ready to drive him away from our *llaqta* forever. After he was gone, would anyone accept the Ugly One as a true shaman?

I whispered, "I don't wish to discuss it."

Chasca put her hand on mine. She didn't probe further.

Watching my sister walk along the path winding away from our village later that day, I was reminded of the *yunka* stranger and how the clouds had hovered about him on this same trail. Now the sky was blue and clear. Inti shone down upon Chasca in approval. I felt the powerful pull of Sacred Sun City on my own being, but it was my sister, unscarred and loved by all, who had been chosen to go there. Her future was a beautiful butterfly unfolding its delicate wings for first flight. I turned away from the sight, not understanding why it was always my place to watch others go to Sacred Sun City while I was left behind.

18
YUYA
Remembering

THE night Chasca left, the dreams began. They were strong dreams, powerful messages. I tossed and turned under the woolen blankets, and Mama told me the next day that I was muttering in my sleep, though she couldn't understand what I was saying. Once I flung my arm so forcefully I hit Sumac and woke us both. He squawked in disapproval, saying, "No. No. No! NO!" as he moved away from me. It was fortunate that Chasca was no longer there. She would have suffered lying next to me in such a state. Night after night the spirits spoke with me, and morning after morning I lay there frustrated, unable to recall their message. The Paqo had requested that I not visit him unless I had a proper reason. Lying under my blankets one night, I realized I was frightened to fall asleep. It wasn't that the dreams scared me, but failing the spirits yet again with my forgetfulness was unsettling. This was a reason, right and true, to see the Paqo. I would visit him the next morning. My decision calmed me, and I was able to close my eyes and sleep.

That night's dream was similar to the others. Perhaps you can guess where it began. I was inside the dark, cool walls of my *huaca*. As before, I felt excited that I would finally meet the spirit that dwelled within. Two jaguar cubs lay dead in a heap in the corner. Mother Jaguar sat next to them, licking their small bodies as if they were still alive. Large tears ran down her face and landed on her children. As her mama tears touched their black fur, the cubs shriveled and shrank. Mother Jaguar cocked her head to the side and watched as the babies changed into a single perfect little toadstool. She lifted her face suddenly and slit her yellow eyes at me. With a low growl, she snarled one word: "Go!"

I awoke with the sound of Mother Jaguar's voice echoing in my head and a feeling of urgency pounding within my heart. Yet, still, I could remember nothing of the actual dream now that I was awake. Rising, I collected Sumac and headed quietly out of the *wasi* to go and see my teacher.

The Paqo was thin. And weary. Sitting across from him, I experienced a new feeling: concern for my teacher. His eyes twinkled as he said, "New Voice, I'm not a dry tree branch, ready to crack in the breeze."

I smiled and looked down. Of course my teacher would be fine. "It's good to see you, Paqo," I said.

He nodded.

"I'm sorry to disturb you. I know you are very busy with the spirits."

He rose and took a pot from the hearth. As he poured two cups of hot tea he said, "I required time alone with the spirits. That time has now passed. All will be fine. The rains will come."

Such good news was completely unexpected. It was a rainbow arcing across a gurgling river. It was flying with Sumac high in the skies. "That's wonderful!" I exclaimed. "When? We must tell the people!"

Sitting down cross-legged in front of me once more, he handed me a cup of tea and took a sip from his own. "It isn't yet time, New Voice. Don't say a word of this to anyone." And here he changed the subject. "The Sapa Inca and his entourage are traveling from the capital city to Sacred Sun City at Machu Picchu. I expect they will reach the roads nearby us sometime tonight or early tomorrow. The emperor intends to hold his Inti Raymi festival in Sacred Sun City this year."

Inti Raymi was the most sacred of festivals. It occurred on the longest night, the night when Inti could choose to leave the people forever. There was much feasting during Inti Raymi. It was a time to pray to the Sun God to come back, and a time to rejoice that he did.

"Will you and I prepare for Inti Raymi here?" I asked, hoping that my teacher and I would be spending more time together now that he was finished fasting with the spirits alone.

The hearth fire hissed and popped in the silence that fell after my question, and the Paqo's face was filled with new lines that spoke of sadness. "I don't think so," he said.

It was as I feared. My sister had left. Sumac was spending more and more time away from me every day. And now it seemed the time of studying with my teacher was through. All my moth ideas had burnt away to nothingness. I would always be the Ugly One, alone and scorned.

"Why are you here, New Voice?"

At the Paqo's words, I suddenly felt as I had the first time I entered his *wasi* and had sat, terrified to be in the presence of such a mighty shaman. The jaguar in the weaving glared at me, as unwelcoming now as it had been back then. Had I ever truly belonged here?

"I have had dreams," I whispered.

"There are three paths to the spirits and Beyond. One such path is through your dreams."

I had come to discuss my failure to recall my dreams, but as usual, my teacher had sent my thoughts in an entirely new direction. "You can reach Beyond through your dreams?"

"Of course."

"Paqo," I said, poised to ask a question I had pondered for some time now, "where is Beyond? Is it past the stars?"

I thought I detected a hint of a smile in my teacher's lips. "I wondered if you would ever ask this. Beyond is not a place. It is all places. It is all times. To visit Beyond is to be everywhere, every time, all at once. It is to be the wind, blowing here and there, a part of everything but invisible to all."

"Have you visited Beyond?"

"I journey there often."

"Will I?"

"Yes."

This simple word gave me much hope. "When?"

"Only you can answer such a question."

I sighed. Of course he wouldn't tell me. "You said dreams are one of three ways to reach Beyond. What are the other two?" I hoped that there might be an easier method. My teacher wasn't usually so flowing with his words. Perhaps he would share a trick with me before he stopped his answers and began his questions.

"Great shamans connect to Beyond through their power. They may use magical plants to help them, or journey unassisted."

I wondered if I had gone to Beyond when I flew with the Handsome One in the sky world. Perhaps the third way was an easier path to Beyond. "And the last way to visit?"

Here my teacher paused. The hearth fire behind him spit and spat. Then he answered. "Death. In death we all become like the wind and reach Beyond."

This didn't sound so simple a path to me. Perhaps my dreams were the best route to Beyond for now.

"Tell me of your dreams," the Paqo said, and I knew he was done telling me of how to reach Beyond.

"There is nothing to tell. I can't remember them." I could hear frustration pushing my voice higher. "I fail the spirits."

The Paqo asked me a question that brought me

again to my first visit to him, for it was one that he had posed that day. "Tell me, what do you remember of your past?"

"Little. Why do you ask me this question?" Here was a difference. Back when we first met, I never would have been bold enough to ask this of my teacher.

"Remembering your dreams, remembering your past, they are as one. The past is the key to the now."

I was about to say that I didn't like my now. I was about to say that my past was gone from my memory, just like my dreams. I was about to say that my future appeared the worst of them all, dark and unhappy. But something in the way the jaguar in the weaving studied me through its slit yellow eyes tickled the inside of my head. I grasped at this faintest of feelings. "Jaguar eyes . . . ?"

My teacher remained silent, waiting for more to come.

"Jaguar eyes. There is a jaguar in my dreams. She shows me something." I closed my own eyes and saw her clearly. She looked downward at an earthen floor. What was it she saw? "A toadstool!" The abrupt sound of my voice scattered any other dream memories I might have pulled from my mind, but I was pleased to finally recall this much. "She showed me a toadstool."

The Paqo nodded his head. "Do you know the significance of the toadstool?"

To see a glowworm in one's dreams meant a loved one would fall ill. If certain birds appeared in dreams, this showed a quarrel would occur in the home. But I didn't know the meaning of the toadstool. I shook my head.

"A toadstool in a dream is an important message from the spirits, New Voice. They are telling you that someone special to you will be making a sacred journey soon."

The Paqo had just said that the emperor was making a sacred journey to Sacred Sun City, but I had never met the emperor. No, my dreams weren't speaking to me about the leader of the Children of the Sun. I knew of whom my dreams spoke. It was my teacher. He would be leaving me very soon. Was he leaving because of the people's fears? Why couldn't he tell them of the coming rains so they would be happy for him to stay? Or was he leaving because of me, because I had failed him in some way?

We faced each other, and the sad lines of his face told me that he knew I understood and he was sorry that our time together had come to an end. Here he gave me my final lesson. "Continue to seek Beyond,

New Voice. Remain open to all. True power can only be held in hands that are open. True wisdom dwells only within a heart that is open. The world speaks only to open eyes, open ears. You have been an excellent student. You are worthy, most worthy."

We stood as one and embraced.

"Goodbye, New Voice."

"Goodbye, Paqo." I barely choked out my last word. *"Pachis."*

That night I did something quite unexpected, I think because I was so sad. When Mama leaned in to kiss me, I didn't turn away. Slowly, as if I were a little rabbit that could be easily startled, she touched her lips to my smooth cheek in a soft Mama kiss. Tears hung in the corners of her eyes. Would she cry and never come near me again? But no, these were tears of joy. Wiping beneath her eyes, she leaned in and kissed me again, this time on my scarred cheek.

"Oh, Mama!" I whispered, and she hugged me to her tightly as we both cried and cried.

I had lost my sister. I had lost my teacher. Finally, on this night, I had gained something. I knew my beautiful Mama would kiss me every night. I felt ashamed, thinking of all the pain I had caused her by turning away time and again, and angry at myself for all the kisses I had missed. Mama had been so patient with me, trying every night. Such is the power of a mother's love. Truly, Mama rivaled Inti himself in her strength.

That night I dreamt more vividly yet. Mother Jaguar growled at me within the *huaca*. "You don't remember me!" she roared.

"They're all leaving me!" I screamed back at her.

Here she paused and licked her paw with one long, deliberate stroke of her thick, pink tongue. She pointed at the toadstool growing out of the earth. "It isn't meant for him," she said.

"Then whose is it?" I asked.

As she and I watched, the fragile growth disappeared from the earth. I held my hands in front of me, and the toadstool lay in my palms like a delicate treasure.

"Yours," she answered. "The sacred journey is yours."

When I awoke, the dream was still there. I could smell the loamy scent of the toadstool on my skin, and Mother Jaguar's voice was strong in the air. The person who was special to me, the person who was to take the sacred journey, was *me,* not my teacher. The Paqo had never said that he was leaving. He had said goodbye knowing it was *I* who would go. I knew then what I was to do, what I *had* to do.

I rose and packed my things as quietly as possible

so as not to awaken my parents. The journey wouldn't be much longer than our travels to Wiñay Wayna had been. I would need the same items. If I left immediately, I could join the emperor's entourage and be in Sacred Sun City well in time for the Inti Raymi festival. I would speak with the Sacred Rock and ask it to remove my scar so I could return home to train with the Paqo and become a shaman, right and true, a shaman whom all the people would accept with open arms and happy hearts. If the Sacred Rock made me whole again, I could have a beautiful future like my sister. It was worth the risk, for what lay ahead for me if I didn't go? Nothing but darkness. Deep inside, I must have known all along that I would be making this journey.

Extra blankets, dried food for myself and Sumac, and a bowl all went into my pack. I glanced at my parents. Father snored quietly. Mama was completely still, peaceful even in her sleep. If my journey was successful, I would return to them as Beautiful Round Face, free from my hideous scar forever. If the emperor allowed me to join his journey. If I was allowed into Sacred Sun City. If I was allowed to speak to the Sacred Rock. If it found me worthy and answered my one request. In my mind, I practiced the words I would say to the Sacred

Rock if I was given the chance. *Will you take my scar away? Will you make me whole again?*

Done packing, I knelt by my sleeping parents. I couldn't tell them. They would stop me. It was upsetting, imagining them awakening to find me gone. But the following sight, the one in which I returned home, beautiful and happy, made me smile. I kissed them both lightly on the cheek and whispered goodbye. Mama lay there so lovely. I hoped that somehow, in her dreams, she heard my words and understood.

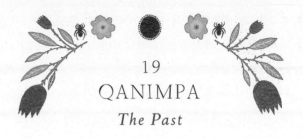

19
QANIMPA
The Past

SUMAC and I found the emperor's entourage just as they were preparing to start the day's travels. I approached cautiously, aware that all my hopes could be ruined at this critical moment. It wasn't uncommon for people to join a group of travelers, even one that included the emperor himself. But the ruler could send anyone away if he so chose, and my face was more than enough reason for him to reject my presence.

There was much commotion as the people packed from the night and prepared to leave. I guessed there to be perhaps thirty in all, but the emperor was nowhere to be seen. Eight men in official patterned clothes moved about a litter, a structure with a wooden base and ceiling surrounded by beautiful hanging cloth. These men were called the feet of the emperor. They carried him in the litter, mounted on poles resting on their shoulders, so he wouldn't tire on his travels. The footmen were large, with hardened faces that clearly spoke of their power. They not only carried the Sapa Inca, they also guarded and protected him.

I thought that perhaps I could join the group without bringing attention to myself, but such was not to be the way. One of the eight footmen sighted me and pointed in my direction. I walked toward him and dropped to my knees at what felt to be a proper distance.

"I wish to join you on this journey," I said in a respectful voice.

"The emperor makes such decisions," he responded. "Remain where you are."

The footman approached the litter and spoke with his eyes averted to the ground. Not even the Sapa Inca's guards were allowed to look upon him from such a close distance. I couldn't hear the response from inside the litter, but I saw the footman making a jagged gesture down his right cheek and knew he was describing me. Another moment passed, and a sandaled foot emerged from the litter. Was the emperor coming to see me? I took in a breath and kept my eyes fixed on a spot on the earth. I would do nothing to insult him, nothing to jeopardize my chances of getting to the Sacred Rock.

I heard feet approaching me on the path and then a slight chuckle. "The Learning Girl."

This was a voice I recognized. I looked up to see the Villac Uma.

"Such a surprised face you show," he said. "I am accompanying the Sapa Inca to Machu Picchu for the ceremony."

I glanced over at the litter.

He answered my look. "Yes, the emperor is inside."

I wanted to study the litter for evidence of the emperor within. But I shook my head to clear my mind. It wasn't the Sapa Inca who should be in my thoughts at this critical point. I remained on my knees and kissed my fingertips in reverence. "Greetings, Villac Uma."

"You may stand," he said. "And you may join the journey."

"*Pachis,* Villac Uma," I said, and I kissed my fingers again as I rose.

"But what of your friend?" he asked.

This question confused me, right and true. "Do you mean Sumac?" I didn't expect the Villac Uma would forbid the bird from joining me.

"No." The priest gestured behind me. "The boy."

I looked where he pointed. A figure was making its way down the trail. At first I wasn't certain who it was, but once I recognized him, I began shaking my head.

Can you guess who huffed and puffed his way toward us? Ucho!

"He doesn't belong here. And he is not my friend," I said in a quiet voice cold with fear.

"The boy serves his purpose," the Villac Uma said. "He joins us as well." Having spoken, he returned to the litter and went inside. I couldn't have argued with him even if he had remained.

By the time Ucho reached the entourage, I had hidden myself within a cluster of people, although I was certain he knew I was there. The footmen lifted the litter, and we began walking. As I took my first steps toward the Sacred Rock, I tried to focus on the request I wanted to make of it. But new questions lodged themselves in my mind like splinters of wood stuck under the skin. Why was Ucho here, and how might he ruin my plans?

The journey to Machu Picchu lasted several days. I spent my time with Sumac, avoiding Ucho and the other travelers as best I could. I didn't see the emperor, and the Villac Uma rarely left the litter. Everywhere I looked, I saw evidence of drought and suffering. Other people slowly joined the group, and there were many hollow cheeks and deadened eyes. One couple leaned against each other as they walked, the woman cradling a limp child in her arms. They wept often to Pachacamac, the creator and giver of life, "Ay! Ay! Let us weep and grieve! Your poor sons are sick of heart. We can offer only our tears in exchange for your showers of rain!" I was so tired of the dust and of the struggle just to get enough to eat. I saw no signs that it would rain as the Paqo had foretold.

It was a journey made in footsteps, in breath that sped when I climbed steep inclines, in sandals and clothes that became covered in dust, in the sweat that dripped down my forehead and neck during the midday strength of Inti's glow, and in the bumps that rose on my skin as I shivered under my blankets during the cold nights. But there was another journey too, an unexpected trip, that took place at the same time. I traveled to my forgotten past. Here is how it happened.

We had crossed a newly repaired hanging rope bridge and stopped for a midday meal. I had so far been able to avoid Ucho and was beginning to wonder if his presence was simply an odd coincidence, if perhaps he had his own reason for being there. But I was far from the protection of my teacher and my home, and I didn't want to tempt Ucho's anger by showing my face. A small group of boulders stood not too far ahead on the path. I walked toward them to eat unseen from the others.

As I rounded one of the large rocks, I came upon a man resting on one of the boulders, the remains of his midday meal scattered about. I was startled to see someone there, but the true surprise came when I realized that it was Hatun, my brother. I don't know which of us was more astonished.

He stood abruptly. "Little Sister? Is that you? Are you a girl or a bird spirit?"

I laughed. With Sumac on my shoulder, I must have looked quite odd to my brother. "I am no spirit," I assured him, and Sumac took off in flight, as if to show he was separate from me. I felt suddenly shy without his presence to cover my cheek, and my hair fell across my scar as if it had a mind of its own.

"Why are you here?" Hatun asked as he came forward and embraced me.

"I'm traveling to Sacred Sun City with the emperor's entourage. Why are you here?"

"I'm traveling home. I expected to see you soon, but not here, not today!"

We settled into the shade of the boulders and talked, filling each other in on the news of the past three years. I told him that Father was as troublesome as ever, that Mama seemed more worried and would be glad to see him, and that Chasca had been chosen to be a Sun Maiden. Hatun described his time laboring on the roads and bridges, and how some of the men had been hard-working while others were lazy. I thought of old Sutic and his snoring ways during planting time. Hatun said he was glad to be going home. He looked forward to starting a family of his own. I studied his strong, handsome face and knew he would have no trouble finding a lovely wife. I was proud of my serious brother who had received praise for his skills and had earned the right to return home in honor to become a full man.

Hatun ended our time together with words that I couldn't have prepared for properly even if I had known they were to come. "There is something I need to say to you, Little Sister," he said. "I have had the opportunity to think a great deal during these past three years. Working on the bridges is mostly time alone with your thoughts. I'm glad the spirits have given me this chance to tell you now. I am sorry. So sorry. I should have said this to you long ago."

Misery etched my brother's face, and I couldn't imagine why he was apologizing to me in such earnestness. He must have recognized my confusion, for he said, "You don't understand? You don't remember?"

"Remember what?"

"It was my fault, Little Sister. I didn't look after you

properly. The jaguar never would have attacked you if I had watched over you as I was supposed to."

I touched my hand to my cheek, tracing the scar lightly with my fingers. Hatun's fault? A jaguar attacked me?

Hatun rushed on. "Ucho distracted me. He was trying to act like the older boys, helping to defend the fields, and he fell and cried out and made a big fuss. I should have let someone else tend to him and kept my eyes on you. I made the wrong choice." He paused, studying my distressed face. "Don't you remember any of this?"

And then . . . I *did* remember. Suddenly, it was there, like a long-ago dream. I was my four-year-old self, playing near the fields as my brother and the other boys slung stones at the birds and other animals that might try to eat the people's precious crops. I wandered off and saw two jaguar cubs. They were playing. I ran to them, wanting to join their fun. There was a growl, then claws and hot animal breath and pain.

"I do remember. A mother jaguar did this to me. I tried to play with her cubs."

"Yes! Yes! It was my fault. I shouldn't have allowed you to wander. Mama asked me to watch you. I should have said this to you long ago, but you were always hiding away from everyone, up on that rock of yours. I thought you didn't want to speak with me, that you were angry with me. It never occurred to me that you had forgotten what happened. Can you forgive me?"

I barely noticed my brother's plea for forgiveness. I was remembering. I was understanding. Already certain I knew the answer, I asked in a rush, "The people, they saved me. What happened to the jaguar?"

"They beat her away and chased her up the mountain. They killed her there by your rock. Her cubs must have died there too."

The Paqo had asked me time and again what I remembered of my past. He had asked me why I had chosen my rock. I finally understood his questions. I could hear his voice echoing in my head. *The past is the key to the now.*

The Mother Jaguar had died near my *huaca*. Her spirit had gone inside. All these years, I had sat with her, the spirit that had changed me from Beautiful Round Face to the Ugly One. She had visited me in my dreams. It was she who had sent me on this journey. Now I was certain I would be allowed to speak with the Sacred Rock and that it would right the wrong done to me when I was a little girl.

Hatun stared at me, his face twisted with worry. But

I wasn't angry with my brother. He wasn't to blame. The gods had placed him on my path so he could show me this piece of my past, so I could walk to Machu Picchu in certainty.

I reached up and placed my hands on his cheeks. "Everything will be fine," I said with a smile. "I'll be fine. I don't know how I forgot all of this. I think I didn't want to remember. But now is the time, right and true, for the past to reveal itself. It will heal me. I'll be fine. Don't worry any longer."

The skin on my brother's face smoothed. He closed his eyes and kissed his fingertips to the sky. "The spirits brought you to me today to lift this burden from me. Travel safely, Little Sister. Until we see each other again."

"Travel safely. Until we see each other again."

Hatun smiled once more and set off down the path. I shielded my eyes from Inti and looked upward. Sumac was circling in a tight arc, as if he was guarding against any possible dangers that might threaten me. Seeing Hatun leave, the Handsome One spiraled down and landed on my shoulder. This was good. I would need his protection, for it was time to do something I had avoided ever since I had become the Ugly One. It was time to confront Ucho.

20
KALLPA
Strength

UCHO was sitting by himself, munching on a dried corn loaf. Good. I wanted to speak with him alone. The sad tree under which he sat had suffered from the lack of rains. The few leaves that dangled from the branches were brown and dead. Ucho's face was similar, dark and empty.

An old habit presented itself as I walked toward Ucho. I shifted my head to the side so my hair would fall over my scarred cheek. Instantly, the world splintered, split by the strands of hair in front of my eye. I felt a quick surge of fear in my stomach. I paused. I didn't want to give Ucho such power over me any longer. It was my turn to claim the strength. With a deliberate motion, I pushed the hair behind my ear and looked up to the sky and Inti for help. I'd once wished I had the power of the clouds, craving their freedom and power to change and move. Now I knew, right and true, that I had changed. I had become Yachachisqa, Learning Girl. And soon I would be Beautiful Round Face once more. I moved like a cloud, gracefully and with the flow of the world, toward Ucho.

His deadened face came to life in a scowl when he saw me. The anger was not to be mistaken, but for the first time I realized that more than hostility lurked within this boy. I thought perhaps his face spoke of frustration and unhappiness. I recalled the day he had been playing the game of *conkana* with Muti and had shown love toward his little brother. I had always viewed Ucho as a tormentor, but what else was he? It was time to find out.

"Why did you come on this journey?" I demanded. I leaned over him, hands on my hips, anger in my voice. Sumac crouched low on my shoulder, his beak open in warning.

Ucho didn't enjoy the way I rose like a mountain before him. That I would approach him and speak so boldly also did not suit my tormentor. He scrambled to his feet but kept his distance from Sumac's large, angry beak.

"I *had* to follow you," Ucho said hotly. "As I told you, I must be in your future. I won't ignore my duty."

I didn't remember Ucho saying this to me, and I

didn't understand what he meant. What duty? I shook my head to clear my thoughts. I wouldn't let him confuse me. I was here to discuss the past, not the future.

"Hatun said you distracted him the day I was attacked by the jaguar."

"It wasn't my fault! I never told the jaguar to attack you!" These words were yelled. Several travelers cast a curious eye toward us, and Sumac flapped his wings and squawked in warning. Ucho lowered his voice. "Why does everyone always say it was my fault?"

"Everyone says? Who is this everyone? All these years, I have never heard a word."

"How could you? They speak of it to me, not to you."

Was it possible that Ucho had suffered because of my scar? Had the people blamed him, caused him grief, because of what had happened to me?

Memories of Ucho thrusting a stick in my side, of Ucho leading other boys as they screeched ugly words to my face, of Ucho throwing dirt at me, crowded about my mind. How dare he claim to be the victim?

"I am the one who suffers! I am the one with the scar!" I said.

"Yes, but I am the one who must marry you and look at you the rest of my life," he retorted.

When I was younger, Mama had given me some

freshly cleaned blankets to carry. The pile was heavy, but she had added another blanket and then another. I bent my knees and told myself I could carry the load, but suddenly it was too much. I buckled under the weight and fell over. Ucho's announcement that he was to marry me was like that last blanket. I had received too many pieces of information this day.

"You? Are to marry me?"

"Of course! That's what our parents have arranged. Why do you pretend not to know?"

Why did everyone assume I knew things that I did not? "I'm not pretending anything. No one told me! Why would our parents make such a horrid arrangement?"

"My parents said it was my fault you were scarred, my fault you would never marry. They promised your family that I would marry you if no one else would. Of course no one else will. You are so ugly. It will have to be me. How could you not know all of this?"

A good question. I had no answer. Perhaps my parents hadn't intended for me to marry Ucho. Or perhaps they were waiting to tell me when I came of age.

Ucho shook his head in confusion. "I thought you knew. I thought you were gloating."

"I wasn't gloating. I was scared of you!"

"And I was angry! I thought you blamed me, and it wasn't my fault. I was a little boy. I shouldn't be punished. I shouldn't have to marry you just because of a small mistake made long ago."

I lifted my chin. "I don't know if I blame you for my scar, Ucho. But all these years you have tormented me, and that *is* your fault."

He remained quiet. I supposed it was too much to expect an apology from Ucho, the Hot Pepper, but at least he wasn't speaking harsh words anymore.

I went on. "Marriage to me would not be a punishment. And why are you so certain I would marry you? I would not. Not if Inti himself commanded it."

Relief and surprise danced on Ucho's face now. "You wouldn't marry me?"

"No. You are not part of my future. Go back home. I don't want you here."

"I can't," he said. "I gave my word."

"I just said you are free. You don't have to honor your parents' promise."

"No. I promised the Paqo that I would make this journey to Sacred Sun City with you."

Another blanket of confusion to add to the pile. "When did you do this?"

"He came to see me the night before you left. He told me you would be making this journey and that I must follow."

I smiled. When the Paqo and I had said our good-bye, I had thought that he was the one who would be making the sacred journey. Not only had he known that it would be me, he also had sent Ucho to keep watch. "I will have to speak with him when I return," I said.

"I don't think you'll be able to. He said he was going back to Cuzco. He said his time in the *llaqta* was over."

A final blanket. Why would my teacher leave our village now? Why would he go to the capital city? Hadn't he been sent away from there in disgrace? I had thought that the Paqo wanted me to go on this journey so I could heal my scar and become a true apprentice to him on my return. Had I misunderstood the spirits' message? No. I knew I was meant to take this sacred journey. But I was fiercely sad to hear that my teacher might be gone when I returned home. Perhaps Ucho was wrong and the Paqo would still be there. Perhaps once I was Beautiful Round Face, he would be my teacher again, and I could learn, right and true, how to help the people.

I understood that Ucho must continue the journey. To deny the mighty Paqo's wishes would be a foolish choice, but I was not pleased. "So we are both going to Machu Picchu," I said flatly.

"We are both going to Machu Picchu," he repeated. His voice wasn't happy either, but at least he didn't grimace at me. For so many years, Ucho and I had been on the opposite sides of a river filled with horrible currents of misunderstanding. I couldn't say we were together in the center of the river now, happily balanced, but the water between us flowed more comfortably.

The people were stirring. It was time to resume walking. My midday meal had been one of information instead of food.

"Why are we going to Sacred Sun City?" he asked.

Picking up my pack, I answered, "To heal the past."

21
MACHU PICCHU
Old Peak
(Sacred Sun City)

I knew Wiñay Wayna was close when I sighted the first hummingbird. It hovered by a nearby branch for a moment before flying over several beautiful orchids and out of sight. The flowers' petals curved coyly around the corners of rocks as if they were trying to peek at who might be passing by. The birds and flowers whispered the message ahead: *The emperor is coming! The emperor is here!*

The litter was carried to a private place in the center of Wiñay Wayna. The rest of us were left to find fountains to cleanse the grime and dust from our travels before entering the holy city. I selected the fountain that gurgled outside the guesthouse where the Paqo and I had stayed, although it was weaker and quieter now. I sighed, thinking of my teacher. Was he already on his way to Cuzco? The possibility that I would not see him again filled me with sorrow and confusion.

I stepped into the fountain. Its water came from a source high above, running through the waterways, emerging from a hole in the rock, and dripping steadily into the small pool in which I stood. I cupped my hands and caught the trickle. It was soft and healing as I rubbed my arms and face with it. I closed my eyes, imagining how this water would feel on my face once the scar was gone.

Sumac drank from the fountain, bobbing his head down and lifting it quickly so the water would flow down his throat. Then he raised his wings and splashed his belly in the water, sending a spray of drops everywhere and cawing in pleasure to be taking such a fine bird bath.

A shell trumpet blew in the distance, calling us back to the trail. It was time to leave. With a hasty scrub to the legs, I stepped out of the fountain and put on my sandals. I hoped I was clean enough, worthy enough, to be allowed to speak with the Sacred Rock.

The final steps of the journey were actual stairs carved out of the mountain. There were one hundred twenty-five in all, and I could hear the labored breathing of my fellow travelers as we climbed. I ached to hurry and reach the city, but I couldn't push past those who walked in front of me, and I wanted to remain gentle and calm. Impatience is a fire that rages in clouded minds, and I needed to be clearheaded. Still, climbing those steps seemed to take longer than the entire rest of the journey.

At last I reached the top. Just ahead was the Sun Gate, the official entrance to the city. The gate was built of stones and arced from one side of the trail to the other. Two guards stood at attention, ready to receive the entourage.

The line of weary travelers extended in front of and behind me on the path. Ucho was toward the back. We hadn't spoken since our conversation near the bridge. For now, we were content to leave each other alone. The emperor's litter was at the very front. The guards kissed their fingertips and bowed deeply from the waist as the eight footmen carried the litter these last few paces of the journey. They paused at the gate, and I saw a yellow-feathered head peek out from behind the cloth. The Villac Uma was speaking with the guards and pointing to the rest of the travelers. I had a sudden fear that he was saying we shouldn't be allowed inside the city, but no, already the litter was in motion again, and the first of the travelers was being questioned by the guards. Soon after, the traveler walked through the gate, and the guards turned to the next person, who was also permitted to pass.

Waiting my turn was another challenge in keeping my mind clear and calm. My heart pounded like drops of rain pummeling down upon the dry earth. I closed my eyes to soothe myself and instead imagined the guards denying me entry. They looked at my ugly face and pointed their fingers back in the direction from which I had come. I opened my eyes. Several more people had walked through the gate. I stepped forward.

At this point, Sumac made a most unusual choice. He took off from my shoulder and headed directly for the guards! With a squawk, he landed solidly on the shoulder of one of them. Why would he select such a critical moment to do something so strange? He had never flown to anyone before, not even to members of my family, and here he was suddenly perched on the shoulder of a complete stranger. I was terrified! All I wanted to do was pass through without being asked too many questions, without bringing too much attention to myself. But the Handsome One had a different understanding of the situation.

All attempts to keep calm fled as I pushed my way

quickly through the waiting people. I had to get Sumac off the guard immediately and beg forgiveness.

Sumac, apparently quite pleased with himself, was bobbing his head at the man as I reached him. The guard surprised me by making the same gesture to the bird. He then turned his helmeted head and looked directly at me. I gasped. These were eyes that I knew. The guard was the *yunka* stranger!

"Sumac Huanacauri has lived up to his name," the *yunka* man said. "He is a handsome rainbow, just as I knew he would be."

The stranger had learned a great deal of the Incan mother tongue in the year since I had seen him. I smiled. "Yes, he is. Thank you for bringing him to me."

He smiled back. "And now he has brought you to me."

I turned my head to the side, feeling suddenly shy. "I didn't come to see you."

"No. Of course not. You have come to speak with the rock."

How could he know? This man was like the Paqo, filled with knowledge of choices before they were made.

"You were able to speak with the rock?" I asked.

"*Ari*. And now I guard Sacred Sun City."

I hoped that the rock was able to answer his

question. I hoped he was pleased with what the rock had said to him.

"Will I be allowed to speak with the rock?" I asked.

"*Ari*. It will happen tomorrow at dawn. Come to the rock then."

I didn't question his answer. He knew of future paths and spoke right and true. Bowing, I kissed my fingertips. "*Pachis*," I said.

"I am not the one to thank. The gods have decided your fate. You will speak with the rock tomorrow." The *yunka* stranger gestured toward the gate.

I held up my arm. Sumac leaped off the stranger's shoulder and landed on mine. Then, with what I hoped was more dignity than childish excitement, I stepped through the stone arch. I couldn't see the city yet, but for the first time I was within its limits. I was worthy. With a final wave to the *yunka* man, I rounded the last of the trail and gazed from the ridge down to Sacred Sun City.

Here I fear my skills as a storyteller will fail me. Have you ever experienced a moment that was so new, a moment of such startling surprise, that you knew it would stay fresh and real in your mind and never leave you for all your days and nights? This was such a moment. I remained as still as the ancient mountains themselves, afraid that if I shifted even a little, the sight before me would disappear. It was too beautiful to exist.

The city was carefully built on the flat top of Machu Picchu, Old Peak. All around, taller mountains loomed like strong guardians protecting the sacred space. Huayna Picchu, Young Peak, rose the closest, like a child who has grown quickly and is standing tall and proud. Another mountain, the Black One, soared higher than the rest, reaching so far into the sky that it need barely whisper and Inti would hear.

There were three clear parts to the city. There was an agricultural section, with terraces cut into the side of the mountain in long, flat steps. There was a large residential area filled with the people's thatched homes. And there was a sacred sector, a complex of temples and palaces, the tallest clearly the emperor's home here in the city. Was he inside, resting from the long journey? Perhaps he was thinking about the Inti Raymi festival, which was to take place beginning the next evening.

The people, they were everywhere. Priests walked about the temples, most of them wearing the golden-yellow feathers that showed their high status. A group of Sun Maidens passed by, moving as one, so beautiful and delicate, they seemed not to walk so much as float. This made me think of Chasca. Perhaps I would see her soon. Then I sighted several noblemen in royal clothing. They sat together on the ground, and two dwarves came over and served them something. I had never seen a dwarf before, but I knew they were special people, sent to the earth marked for this sacred life of duty to the nobility.

Clouds drifted in and out among the temples and structures as if they were trying not to disturb the quiet peace of this place. Birds swooped just below me, playfully dipping and then rising on the air currents. I watched as one soared higher and higher. To fly alongside would be a journey to Beyond, but I remained solidly on the earth.

Here is what I want you to know of Sacred Sun City. Power moved in this place. I could hear it crackling within my head and whispering with its forever-voice in the wind. I could feel it radiating out of the very rocks and earth. Ancestors and spirits dwelled everywhere, pleased to be within the city's walls. *Welcome. I have been waiting for you,* the city said to me. And somewhere nearby, the Sacred Rock sat. I could feel it pulsing with energy, calling out to me.

Tomorrow morning, I told it in my mind. *Tomorrow morning I will come to you to be healed and made whole.*

22
WILLKA RUMI
Sacred Rock

I claimed a small, empty *wasi* on the outskirts of the residential area and placed my pack and blankets within. I didn't spend any time arranging my temporary home. Instead, I wandered throughout the city with the Handsome One riding proudly on my shoulder. The Apurimac River, the Great Speaker, gurgled far below along the base of Machu Picchu mountain. From such a distance, the river looked like a thin band of silver or a sparkling snake that slithered its way across the land. Evergreen trees grew along the sides of the surrounding mountains, but the forest of the valley below appeared no larger than bits of lichen and twigs.

My wanderings took me to a place near the Sacred Rock. *It is just around that bend*, I was told. But I already knew that. I could feel its presence. However, I chose not to go to it. An understanding deep within me told me I wasn't to meet the rock until sunrise. To turn and walk away was not easy. The pull of the Sacred Rock was strong. It breathed itself into my being and held on to my heart with a simple, insistent force.

I kept to myself throughout the day but tried to see all. The Paqo had once told me, the more one was aware of the outer world, the more one was aware of the inner world. I wished to know both. I saw enormous puma and condor statues carved from solid rock. Small *cochas,* perfect circles cut into the stone base of the city, held pools of still water that reflected the sky above. It was an odd sensation, to stare down at one's feet and see moving clouds.

There were fewer signs of the difficult times here in Sacred Sun City. Of course the emperor would be sure to care for so powerful a place. Its precious fields would be watered with the last drops gathered. Its priests and nobles would be fed the last grains of the storehouses.

I watched llamas in the fields chewing grass. A shepherd boy who reminded me of the handsome Acoynapa of Uncle Turu's story played a flute to the grazing animals. The sound lifted up to the skies in a way that filled me with a simple sadness. A group of nobles sat and debated scholarly issues. Another group of men toiled in a quarry, extracting large rocks. Twice I saw Sun Maidens walking about in pairs, but I didn't spy my sister, and I was afraid to approach them and ask where she might be.

I didn't eat. I wanted to approach the Sacred Rock light and empty.

Twilight fell quickly. Activity stopped as the people ended the day's work. I made my way back to the *wasi* and unpacked the few items I had brought. I decided to use my favorite wool blanket, the beautiful red one with weavings of the sun and the birds, as the hanging for the entrance. I preferred this blanket for sleeping, but at some point during the day I had realized I would not be sleeping this night. Perhaps it was a certain nervousness that kept my heart beating slightly faster than normal. Perhaps it was the energy of the city. But when the heart doesn't slow for rest after Inti sets, it is best to honor its wishes.

Sumac's heart gave him no such instructions. He was already settling down on a smaller weaving on the floor in a corner of the *wasi*, his head tucked into the soft feathers of his back, his body scrunched low to hold in its warmth. He was grating his beak comfortably and occasionally mumbling his bird version of Mama's humming tune.

I went outside and lay on the earth, staring

upward. The tall mountain, the Black One, commanded my attention. I stared at its pointed tip in quiet wonder. It held many secrets within its huge body, and it seemed to be lonely, although it was surrounded by other mountains. Perhaps its knowledge and wisdom kept it separate, like a shaman living on the edge of a *llaqta*, feared by the people.

Above the looming outlines of the mountains, the children of Inti and Mama Killa twinkled in the dark sky, a familiar sight in such an unfamiliar place. Perhaps because of Sumac's humming, thoughts of my own mama came to me. Was she thinking of me just then? Was she looking up at the skies and hoping that I was all right? I took comfort in the knowledge that the Paqo would have told her where I had gone, and that Hatun would be with her by now. Would Mama understand the reason for my journey? Perhaps she was excited, thinking of her youngest child returning home healed and beautiful, ready to resume her training to become a shaman, right and true.

I closed my eyes and imagined Mama here with me, leaning over my face and giving me a good-night kiss. I had remembered many things from my past on this journey, but I still couldn't recall the time before my scar, when I must have accepted Mama's kisses with little-girl delight. I had only one true memory of my mother kissing me, the night before I had left on my journey. I was grateful to have that one.

⊡⊡

Just before dawn, I stretched and headed toward the Sacred Rock, Sumac groggily perched atop my shoulder. Now that it was time to speak with the rock, my heart slowed. Waiting can be more challenging than doing. The city was still. There was a heavy feeling in the air, and I noticed dark clouds hovering above like angry jaguars waiting to pounce. I walked as silently as possible, not wanting to break the spell of the quiet night.

I paused where I had stood the day before. It was time. It was finally time. Hushed voices whispered nearby. Smoothing my wrap and running my fingers through my hair to neaten it, I took a deep breath and released it slowly. *Here I am,* I thought as I made the last steps around the path to meet the rock.

Welcome, it seemed to say as I laid my eyes upon it for the first time. It was almost twice as tall as I, with a flat surface and a pointed tip. Immediately, I knew I had seen it before. *Yes, we met last night,* it agreed. *Look behind me.*

The Sacred Rock had been cut and shaped to look

exactly like the Black One, which rose directly behind it. It was a miniature version of the mighty, lonely mountain I had compared to a powerful shaman the night before.

Several people stood with the guards about the base. Some whispered with each other. Others were silent.

"Here is the way of the Sacred Rock," one of the guards announced to the small group of assembled people. The wind began to blow, and he raised his voice further to be heard. "We will tell you when it is your turn to speak with the wise one. You will approach it alone and ask it your question. It may answer. It may tell you something else rather than addressing your question. Or it may choose not to speak with you at all. Such is the way of the rock. When you are done, move away so the next person may have an opportunity. You," he said, pointing to an older man with a stooped back and a wooden cane, "will speak first."

Trembling, the man bowed his head. I could see the pain of hunger in his shrunken body. He held a handful of small rocks and dried flowers, and here I realized I had made a critical error. I had not thought to bring a gift for the rock! Did I have time to fetch something? No. Then, what could I offer that would hold meaning? How could I demonstrate my complete faith in its power to heal me?

The old man stepped away from the rock. His face spoke of much happiness. Of course the rock had spoken well with him. He'd remembered to bring it an offering! The guards pointed to a woman who carried a scrawny newborn secured to her chest. She bowed and approached. Was she asking the rock for food for her child? To heal a sickness? How many of these people were here because of the troubles brought on by the drought?

Inti was beginning to rise. The Sun God was battling the large clouds that now filled the sky world, and I didn't take it as a good omen when the first faint flickers of his rising body were abruptly covered. Sumac stirred with these feeble signs of the dawn. He preened, his left wing lightly touching my scarred cheek. His feathers had kept the world from having to gaze upon the ugly side of my face, and they had freed me from the constant worry of covering it. Thinking of how I had hidden myself, I had the perfect idea, right and true. I knew how to show my faith in the Sacred Rock's ability to heal me. But how could I do it properly?

I looked about me. One of the waiting men had a

knife hanging from his belt. It was an ordinary one, not a *tumi*, but it would do. He was staring at the rock with intense concentration, lines that spoke of troubles etched into his face.

I tiptoed to him and leaned in. "May I borrow this?" I asked.

"What?" he asked in surprised distraction.

"May I borrow your knife? I'll return it right away."

He lifted it from its sheath and handed it to me, not bothering to say anything more.

I looked at Sumac, my friend, my protector, my companion and guide to Beyond. "You are a true friend, and I thank you for all that you have done for me. But you must go now," I whispered. He stopped preening to look at me. I studied him as well, the white crinkled skin surrounding his dark brown eyes, the splendor of the individual red feathers. I knew this bird so well.

"Go. I must do this without you," I said, and with a quick bob of his head, the Handsome One took off in flight. He circled once and then headed in the direction of the *wasi*.

I lifted the knife. With a sense of ceremony and purpose, I placed the sharp edge against my hair, held it taut with my other hand, and began to cut in short, powerful motions. My long, beautiful black hair that had served as my shield from the world came away in large clumps. I tried to hold the strands carefully, not wanting to drop any on the ground. I did my best to shorten the haircut evenly, just below my chin. When I was done, I handed the knife back to the man. He didn't even look at me as he placed it back in its cover, so intently was he focused on the rock.

I flipped my head from side to side, trying out the new feeling of lightness. The woman with the baby was finished. The guards pointed to the man with the knife, and he stepped forward. His lips were moving. He was already in conversation with the rock. I realized he had probably been speaking with it the entire time, and I hoped my interruption hadn't troubled him.

I clutched my cut hair tightly as I watched the people selected one by one to speak with the rock. I knew many of them were feeling desperate — for food or for the healing of an illness in themselves or a loved one. I wished I had the power of the rock, the power to heal them all.

Somehow I knew I was to go last. Soon enough there were two of us remaining. I eyed the young man who waited with me. He shifted from foot to foot.

When the guards pointed to him, he offered me a nervous smile before he went to the rock.

"You are calm," a voice spoke from behind me.

I turned. It was the Villac Uma! I dropped to my knees and kissed my fingertips. I wanted to ask why he was there, but it would have been presumptuous to do so. I'm certain he heard my unspoken question, but he didn't offer me an answer. Instead, he raised his eyebrows and gestured with his head. "The rock waits for you."

My body, the entire world, seemed to turn suddenly cold at these words. The young man was gone. The guards were watching, waiting to see what I was going to do.

I rose and approached the Sacred Rock carefully, as I would a baby jaguar with whom I wished to play. In my mind I practiced one last time what I would say. *Will you take my scar away? Will you make me whole again?* Fingers trembling, I placed my cut hair on the earth in front of it, and the wind immediately snatched up my offering and scattered it to the sky world. Pushing my shortened hair behind my ears, I stepped onto the ledge at the base of the rock and placed my hands against its cool surface. Rich green lichen grew on its body. I leaned in, touched my scarred cheek to the stone, and looked up at its pointed tip. Behind it, the Black One loomed, mirroring its shape.

I closed my eyes and took a deep breath. And here something astonishing happened. "Please," I said as I exhaled, "please, will you bring the rains to the people? Will you make the crops grow so the people can be whole and healthy again?"

The words that I had spoken surprised me to my very core. I opened my eyes in panic. What had I just done? Before I could correct myself and speak the words I had come to say, the Sacred Rock was responding. The winds swirled about, and the earth rumbled deep and low, telling of its thirst for the waters that hadn't come for so long. Then a loud clap of thunder echoed from the dark clouds. Illapa had finally thrown his stone at his sister's water jug, and it released a torrent of rain that pelted down all about me.

I fell to the ground, and the rain was so powerful, it seemed to be pushing me into the thirsty earth as it tried to soak up every drop the clouds offered. I stared at the Sacred Rock, my tears mixing with the rain as they streamed down my cheeks, one smooth, one still hideously scarred. I had lost my only chance to heal myself, right and true, for I knew the rock would never answer a second request.

The ground was muddy and cold. Several strands of my cut hair swirled round and round in a churning pool of dirty water. I grabbed a fistful of mud and ground it into my scar as I shook with hot sobs.

Strong hands pulled me to my feet, and I was staring at the Villac Uma. It took all my control to face the powerful head priest at such a moment.

"Apprentice Girl, did you speak to the rock of rain?"

What a person said to the rock was sacred and private. This would have been too bold a question from anyone but the Villac Uma.

"I meant to ask it to take away my scar. I don't know why I asked for the rains. It was a mistake! I made a mistake!"

The mighty shaman raised his arms to the skies, and the winds quieted, as if he had commanded them to do so in order that he might speak. Even the rain sounded apologetic as it fell around us, tiptoeing its way to the earth. "It was no mistake," he said. "The Sacred Rock has served you well."

I concentrated on the Villac Uma's moving lips, trying to stay with his words. But I didn't understand what he meant. I clenched my hands together. The nails dug into my palms.

"We have known for some time that this drought

would happen. We also knew that a young girl would rise to power and appease the spirits, but it would have to be the proper girl, right and true. The spirits told us this girl would be marked by one of their own so we would know her." Here the Villac Uma raised his arm and traced his finger along my scar, reminding me of that long-ago day when the *yunka* stranger had done the same.

"The Paqo and I were both rising priests in the capital city. We knew one of us was destined to be the Villac Uma and the other was to find the Marked Girl and be certain she was the one. When we heard of a little child who had been scarred by a jaguar, the Paqo chose to move to her village to watch over her and be certain she was strong enough to follow her destined path. That child was you, Marked Girl."

I couldn't accept that my teacher had kept such secrets from me, had allowed me to suffer as I had. "He knew? The Paqo knew all of this? Why would he keep this from me?"

"You had to find your voice and learn the way, the path of helping the people. We were watching to see if your choices showed us you were indeed the Marked Girl." The priest lifted his hands toward the Sacred Rock in reverence. "You came to Sacred Sun City and spoke with the rock. You asked it the true question of your heart. It responded to you and gave us the rain. Marked Girl, you are the one we have sought, right and true. The jaguar marked you so there would be no mistake. If you so choose, you will study with me and become a shaman priestess, a mighty shaman priestess." The Villac Uma smiled down at me as a father would a child. "Do you accept the fate the spirits have handed you, Marked Girl?"

I was too overwhelmed to speak. The tears returned as I nodded a disbelieving yes. The nod became more vigorous, chin to chest and then to the sky. I wanted no confusion in my answer. Yes! Yes! Yes!

The powerful priest smiled in true joy. "The feast tonight is in honor of Inti, but it will also be in honor of you. Try to rest now. We will celebrate all night, and you will begin your training and duties with me at dawn. You will swallow the sacred drink and journey to Beyond to assist me in the ceremony."

The Villac Uma left me then. I dropped to my knees the moment he was gone from sight, unable to hold my own weight any longer. I was the Marked Girl, worthy of studying with the Villac Uma himself? It seemed an impossible thing. There must have been a mistake.

No, the Sacred Rock whispered. *There is no mistake, Marked One. You will become a most powerful priestess.*

I crawled to its base through the mud and rain and placed my hand against its rough body once more. *You are worthy, most worthy,* it reassured me. I bowed my head, trying to accept its message with grace and gratitude. I was worthy.

23
KACHITU
Beauty

YOU might not think I could sleep upon finding out I was the Marked Girl. But I had stayed awake the night before, and speaking with the rock and then the Villac Uma had left me exhausted. True, nagging worries filled my head. What if I drank the sacred drink and didn't go to Beyond? Would Inti refuse to rise? Would the Villac Uma decide not to train me? I had sought Beyond and had failed time and again. How could I find it on command during the Inti Raymi festival? I told these worries to hush, that it was my sacred duty to be well rested and refreshed when the evening's festivities began. I walked back to the *wasi* in an exhausted trance. Sumac was nowhere to be seen. I lay upon the floor and fell into a deep sleep.

Mother Jaguar came to me in my dreams and spoke

tenderly. "Come. Play with my children." The two cubs were frolicking in the corner of the cave. I crept to them slowly, wanting to surprise them. With a fast pounce, I caught the tail of one and the hind leg of the other. They spun and nipped at me playfully. The larger of the two nudged my forehead with his own, a tender cat caress of friendship. In this way, I was finally able to play with the cubs that I had approached when I was four.

"Thank you," I said to Mother Jaguar. "Your children are lovely."

I awoke from this dream abruptly. Two Sun Maidens were kneeling over me, gently shaking my arms to rouse me. Their faces were so beautiful, the cloth of their dresses so fine, the scent of their perfume so delicate, I was unsure what to do or say. I jolted upward, swinging my head to cover my cheek with my hair. Too late I remembered I had cut off my long, flowing strands and couldn't shield my scar from their gaze. I would like to say that I was at peace with this shorter hair, but I felt horribly exposed and uncomfortable.

"Marked Girl," one of them said in a hushed voice. "We have come to prepare you."

The other Maiden smiled warmly, and I realized it was my very own sister, Chasca! We beamed at each other and embraced. To have her with me, to see her again, was a gift from the gods. I said nothing as each of them took one of my hands. I hoped Chasca and I would have the chance to be alone together, but now was not the time to talk.

The rains had stopped while I slept. The three of us walked as one to the Acllahuasi, the Sun Maidens' convent, and the air was full of the fresh, earthy smell that a strong rain leaves. The Acllahuasi was a blur of beautiful faces and fine scents and giggling voices. A group of Maidens gathered around me in a room filled with cloth and jewelry. They studied me intently, discussing how best to present me. Chasca stayed by my side the entire time.

An older Maiden stepped forward with an air of authority. "I am Ocllo."

I nodded to her, not sure what name to offer. Finally, I said, "I am the Marked Girl."

She accepted the name. "The hair"—she pointed to my head—"must be evened. And I think braided would be best. Let us cleanse her first."

They led me to a fountain. I stripped off my dirty travel wrap and stepped in. The water was soothing and abundant. In a year of no rains, this was the most luxurious of baths.

One of the Maidens said, "This water flows from the direction of your home *llaqta*. It will make your skin soft and glowing."

Hands rubbed me with pumice and scented cleansers. Oils were rubbed into my hair and skin. The Maidens used a small knife with an ornately embellished golden handle to cut and smooth my hair, and many hands began twining small strands into a series of formal hanging braids.

I could see from her demeanor that Chasca was still adjusting to her new life. This Sun Maiden world of baths and fine jewelry and formal hair weaving was foreign to her, and she was no longer the prettiest girl whose beauty demanded the attention of everyone around her. Was she happy here? And how had she felt when she heard that I was the Marked Girl? Again I hoped we would have time together without the others hovering about.

"Now the clothing," Ocllo said. Several dresses of finely woven cloth were brought out. Some had beautiful patterns of red and yellow lines crisscrossing the fabric. Some had feathers or shells woven into the designs. "Which do you like?" she asked me.

I was to choose? They were all so lovely! Shyly, I pointed to one with red feathers woven across the chest, in honor of Sumac.

The Maidens nodded in approval and slipped it onto my body. Never had I felt material so soft. Someone secured a necklace of large red oyster shells around my neck, and a broad bracelet of silver was pushed onto my wrist. One of the Maidens draped a shimmering shawl about my shoulders and secured it with a shining golden *campu*. Someone else placed a headdress of pure white feathers atop my head. In the center, a lone golden feather, the mark of a new shaman, stood tall and bright. Soft sandals were placed in front of my feet, and I stepped into them.

"Here, attach this at your side," Ocllo said, handing me a *koka* bag made entirely of red feathers. "The Villac Uma will give you the dried leaves that all shamans carry, and you can place them inside."

I nodded and secured the bag at my hip.

The Maidens stepped back to look at me. I was self-conscious under their scrutiny. The clothes and scents and jewelry were lovely and special, but I was the same girl underneath all this finery. I still felt like the Ugly One. My scar was completely exposed, and it took all my will not to cover my cheek with my hand.

Ocllo came toward me. "May I?" she said with her arm extended. She was asking to touch my scar. Of course I didn't want her to, but how could I refuse?

With all the Maidens watching and my sister holding my hand protectively, Ocllo reached a tentative finger to my face and rested it on the corner of my eyebrow. Her touch was soft and curious as she followed the mark down my face to the corner of my mouth. "It looks like the Apurimac River," she said with awe in her voice, and the others nodded their heads in agreement. "You are lucky the spirits have touched you so. Every girl here wishes she were the one to have been marked in such a sacred manner."

This was too much to accept. I bowed my head.

"Are you ready?" Ocllo asked me.

"Yes," I said. I was nervous, but I was also eager to begin the night's festivities. I tried not to think of what was required of me just before dawn.

24
INTI RAYMI
Festival of the Sun

IN a rush of fluttering hands and laughter, the Maidens and I went outside to the central area of the city. It was a large field near the temples in which the people could gather.

Inti had set, and dozens of fires rose up into the night sky, burning so powerfully that they lit the field almost as if it were daytime. They reminded me of the mighty fire that had bitten its keeper at the Gathering. Each of these fires had a keeper as well. The huge blazes were meant to light the way during this longest night of the year, so Inti would see the path to come back to us. They were a flaming invitation to the Sun God not to abandon his children forever.

Drums beat insistently, and wooden flutes cast their haunting spells on the many people gathering in the field. They were all dressed in their finest clothing and jewelry, strutting about and feeling joyful on this celebratory night. Aromas of freshly cooked food wafted about, intermingling with the scent of the sweet woods burning in the fires.

In a year of such drought, taking a bath as I had done was a luxury, but it was nothing compared with the feast that evening. There were foods I had never seen or smelled or tasted—a strange creature called a shrimp and some sort of rare fish. Platters of duck and partridge, rabbit and bird eggs, and seasoned venison passed by in dizzying numbers. Kidney beans, peanuts, green and red chili peppers, sorrel, cress, and quinoa, yucca and cucumbers, and of course potatoes and corn were piled, steaming, into the people's bowls. There was honey, fat, and vinegar to spice each dish. Sweet plums and bananas and rough-skinned cherimoyas spilled over the edges of rush mats, ready for the taking. Not a single morsel would be dropped to the ground or go wasted, for it was said that if the food were able, it would weep tears at being misused in any manner.

The people did not misuse the food. Such a grand feast was appreciated by all as they sat in groups about the fires, scooping large helpings and licking their fingers. *Aca* flowed in abundance, adding more laughter and happiness.

I thought of the meager Inti Raymi meal the people back home would be scrambling to put together. They would smile and pretend that all was fine, but it would be no feast. How lovely it would be if Mama and Papa and Hatun could be here with us. I wished all the Incan people could rejoice on this sacred night with such a bountiful celebration.

Chasca and I walked with the Sun Maidens. They were excitedly pointing here and there, calling out to one another to try this, sample that, look at this unusual color, see how that one steams in its dish just so. I chose some familiar foods and a few new items, but I was too nervous to eat much. The people kept glancing at me from the side, trying to view the Marked Girl who had brought them the rains. Many smiled at me if they managed to catch my eye. It was an odd sensation, to receive so much attention, to be so admired, after a lifetime of rejection and scorn.

Chasca took my hand and we moved away from the others. We sat alone to eat and talk, to be sisters together.

"You look beautiful!" she gushed as she settled herself next to me on a rush mat. "How do you feel?"

"Wonderful," I replied, but something in my tone caused my sister to pause and study me intently.

"What's troubling you?" she asked in concern.

"Nothing. What could possibly be wrong?" I replied in what I thought was an innocent voice.

Chasca laughed. "Don't try to fool me, Micay. I was there when you were born!"

I tried to smile at my older sister, but my face faltered. "Chasca, this all seems so impossible. What if everyone is wrong? What if I'm not the Marked Girl? What if I can't travel to Beyond at the ceremony? What if I fail the people? What if all I have ever truly been and ever will be is the Ugly One?"

"They chose right and true," Chasca replied in a fierce tone. "Do you think the Villac Uma could make such a mistake?"

I had reassured myself with the very same thought.

"And," Chasca added, "the rains came when you asked for them, didn't they? I have always known that your path was special. Sacred. I've told you this before. You didn't believe me, but I knew."

I thought back to the time Chasca had found me covering my face with mud, trying in vain to hide my scar. She had said, even then, that I was special. Perhaps she truly *had* known all along. I reached over and took her hand as I offered a simple smile of gratitude. She squeezed back, the strength in her touch telling me how deeply she believed in me. It was true that here in Sacred Sun City, Chasca was one of many lovely Sun Maidens, but in my eyes she had an inner beauty that shone the most brightly of all.

"You're glad it is I and not you who spoke to the gods," I said.

She laughed. "Yes. It's enough for me to be the sister of the Marked Girl. I would prefer to catch the eye of a handsome nobleman."

"Have you seen any you like?" I asked.

"A few," she mused. "But the most handsome man I have seen so far is one of the llama herders!" She covered her mouth and giggled. "I don't think Ocllo will allow me anywhere near him, though. She takes her position as our supervisor very seriously."

I laughed. Poor Ocllo. If my sister set her heart on someone, it would be difficult to keep her from what she wanted. I wondered what the outcome of my sister's romantic adventures would be. Would she marry? Would she be happy?

"Chasca, are you glad you are here?"

She nodded her head slowly. "There have been some challenges, true. But there have been many, many good things. I know I will lead a happy life."

We stared at each other, each of us thinking about our future path.

"I'm very proud of you," I said.

She held me to her. "I'm very, very proud of you."

We stayed this way for some time, two sisters clasped in a motionless embrace that spoke of love, of pride, of friendship.

Storytellers began to gather at the fires. Some of the people flocked to them, attracted to their laughter and fun. They gestured broadly with their arms and made expressive faces, reminding me of Uncle Turu. Other people had begun dancing to the steady beat of the many drummers.

"I want to dance! Will you join me?" Chasca asked with a gleam in her eyes.

I smiled. If I couldn't dance tonight, when could I? "Yes," I said. "But you go now. I'll join you soon."

"Micay!" she began to protest.

"I will. I promise. I just want to sit and watch for a while."

My sister gave me a stern glance before she leapt up to join the dancers. I lingered behind and nibbled on my food, content to watch for now as the festivities continued.

"May I join you?" It was Ucho, my longtime enemy, requesting permission to sit with me. He held a plate of food, and his face was uncertain.

"Of course," I said.

He sat. The pounding of the drums filled the empty silence of Ucho's discomfort. "You, ahhh, you look very nice," he said at last.

If someone had told me Ucho would be saying such words to me, I would have called this person a liar.

"Thank you," I whispered. We both looked down in embarrassment.

"When I return to the village, I'll tell the people you're the Marked Girl, that you're to become a sha-man."

If I travel to Beyond, I thought to myself, but I didn't share my fears with Ucho. I imagined him arriving home with the news. How would he tell the people? How would they receive the announcement? Would they believe him? Would they cheer for me?

"Thank you," I repeated.

A sudden breeze announced Sumac's approach. I smiled and held out my arm for my friend, who landed with grace. Ucho flinched at his presence, but Sumac chose to ignore him. Instead, the bird squawked hap-pily at me, as if to say, *Hello, here I am, how are you, and what have you been doing this fine evening?*

The *yunka* man followed Sumac to us. He sat down next to me. Ignoring Ucho much as the bird had, he said, "The Handsome Rainbow and I have enjoyed each other's company today."

"I wondered where my feathered friend had been."

"He found me early this morning. It has been a good day we have had together."

Sumac bobbed his head and squawked his general happiness, then fluttered to the ground and began eating the food from my dish. Of course he began with the steaming pile of corn. I slid back slightly, not wanting his usual messes to land on my beautiful dress.

I could hear the drums pounding more loudly, speaking quite clearly to me. *Dance!* They screamed. *Dance! Dance!*

"I told my sister I would join her," I said, and Ucho, Sumac, and the *yunka* man all nodded as I rose to find Chasca.

I sighted her easily enough, dancing next to one of the many drummers. The drummer's hair was a black blur as he beat on the instrument. His entire being moved with the intricate rhythms he pounded with his hands. I watched, entranced, and my body began to bob up and down in time with his movements. I started to sway, and soon enough I was turning round and round, just as I had seen Chasca do so many times, just as she was doing right now, her smile a beautiful offering to the sky above. I used to watch my sister with deep envy as she danced with such abandon. Now I would join her.

I held my hands up to the sky. The stars blurred as I twirled faster and faster, gazing upward as I spun, and they smiled back down at me in happiness. Such freedom, to dance! Why had I never done this before? My braids lightly slapped my cheeks each time I slowed or sped up. My heart beat wildly, as if it were the only thing that existed. It drowned out the sound of the drums. It *became* the drums as it pounded its own pulsing rhythms into the night.

Time ceased to have meaning. I could have danced forever. It felt as if I had. But then Ocllo was before me, holding a golden bowl.

"The Villac Uma has sent this sacred drink for you, Marked Girl," she said. "It is to prepare you for the ceremony and your journey to Beyond."

Already it was time for the sacred drink? My stomach flipped and flopped in fear.

She handed the bowl to me. It was filled to the brim with a strong-smelling liquid. She said, "It is a mixture of *aca* and *koka* and other sacred plants. Drinking it will begin your journey as a shaman priestess."

I held the bowl to my lips and tasted a small drop. It was not pleasant, but I could feel its sacred power. I took several gulps.

"Slowly," Ocllo said.

I nodded. I would drink it with reverence.

Ocllo watched as I took sip after sip of the mixture. I didn't grimace, though it was increasingly strong in its flavor. But a curious thing began to happen as I neared the bottom of the bowl. The taste was not so objectionable. My senses switched, and the sound of the drums became the taste of the drink. The light of the fires jumped and danced, and the people sitting around the storytellers were boulders rising from the earth. The stars giggled in the sky, and I joined them. Oh, we had such a good laugh!

I vaguely felt Ocllo pushing the bowl to my lips, and I finished the rest of the drink.

The Villac Uma appeared as if from nowhere. "Marked Girl," he whispered in a voice that seemed almost too slow and deep for me to understand, "it is time for the ceremony."

I walked carefully, concentrating on each step so as not to fall, the head priest guiding me with his steady hands. The people looked at me, but their faces were a blur. I smiled, hoping they could see how happy I was, how honored.

There was the white rock with the golden ropes tied tightly to it in order to capture the sun and hold him firmly to the world. The priest leaned in closer yet to me. His breath smelled of *aca,* and shadows from the fire moved on his face in quick rising-and-falling motions, so it seemed as though Inti were waking and setting on the holy man's face over and over again. His dark eyes reflected the hypnotic, dancing flames.

The people pressed in all about us. Their energy pulsed through me in overwhelming waves as they moved their hands and bodies in excitement. I tried to distinguish among the faces. They were so close, then far away, then close again. Was that Ucho I saw right in front of me? Was that my sister next to him? No, it was an old lady. Her mouth was moving in prayer as she kissed her fingers and pointed at me and then at the sky. And yes, my sister was there too, next to the old lady. Their bodies were so close, their forms blurred. Chasca's face spoke of great pride. I tried to smile at her, but I wasn't certain my mouth was mine to control any longer.

Behind the white rock, I spotted a carved stone jaguar. It hissed near the fires and wouldn't stop looking at me. The Villac Uma's lips were moving, but I couldn't understand what he was saying. He placed one of the golden ropes into my hands. I knew what I was to do. It was my sacred duty to help the head priest pull the Sun God back to the world.

The rope was thick in my hands, and I could feel the holy prayers that it held. With all the energy and love I could offer from my being, I pulled alongside the head priest, pleading for Inti to rise and join us in another year.

Inti's first beams shone brightly and abruptly, striking the very center of the stone jaguar's eye and giving him a fiery fierceness. The Villac Uma dropped the rope to the ground, and I followed his gesture. He raised his hands high and proclaimed, "Praise Inti! The Sun God has returned to us once more!" I lifted my arms to the sky in praise and prayer, as did all the people. The entire world was a blur of light and warmth. The earth below looked so beautiful, so loving and comfortable.

As Inti's rays showed strong and true, the power of the sacred drink overcame me. I fell to the ground in exhaustion, and the earth received me with an embrace. And here a very strange thing happened. I floated above myself. Not high in the sky world, as I had when I'd joined Sumac in flight, but closer to the earth and to my body. I watched in confusion as the people stopped their prayers and looked at my crumpled form in hushed fear. Chasca screeched and ran to me, placing her hands on my face and shoulders, shaking me and yelling my name. All of this I saw from above.

The Villac Uma stood next to my fallen self. He gazed from my body to the people. "The Marked Girl is fine," he announced. "She has gone on a sacred journey to Beyond. She is as the wind, able to travel to all times and places. She will return when her journey is complete."

Chasca was crying onto my cheeks, but I felt none of her tears on my skin. At the head priest's words, she looked up. "She isn't dead?"

The Villac Uma shook his head solemnly. "No, she is not. Bring her to the Acllahuasi and make her comfortable. She will return to her body in good time." Here the mighty shaman paused. His dark eyes narrowed as he turned his gaze to me — not to my body, but to the me that hovered above the ground, and he offered a subtle smile. "Although before one returns, one must first journey," he went on. "Strange, to be able to travel anywhere, anytime, and to choose to remain still."

I waited only until I saw that Chasca and Ocllo had carried my body safely to the Acllahuasi. They moved me tenderly, as they would a sacred mummy, and placed me on a heap of luxurious weavings in a private room. My body self was safe. I was free to journey as the wind. Come and see where I went and what I saw in Beyond.

25
HANAQ
Beyond

IMAGINE you are as one with the world, with all times, all places. Where would you go? When would you go? Listen and I will tell you of all the wonderful places and times I see in Beyond as the ever-blowing, ever-moving wind.

First I travel to my future. As the wind, I watch myself journey to Cuzco with the Villac Uma to study the ways of the shaman. He teaches me the language of the stars and the *koka* leaves and the secrets of Beyond. I wipe away the many tears of the people. I speak with Inti and Illapa on their behalf and there is much, much rain for the earth. The Paqo, my old teacher, is there as well. He is a powerful priest who has returned to the capital city and is treated with the utmost honor and respect for having found the Marked Girl. With the Villac Uma and the Paqo as my guides and companions, I become a third power in the Incan empire. The people know my name, and I grow to become the Marked Woman. I see the people kiss their fingertips and bow in reverence as I walk by. It is a future full of hard work and dedication, but it is a good future, a good life, that I see.

Now I see the future of my family. Ucho travels home and tells the people of what happened to me at Sacred Sun City. Mama cries when she is told I won't be returning, but she is smiling with pride as the tears flow down her cheeks. Hatun is home now, and his presence helps to heal Mama's sadness over my absence. My brother marries and has three daughters. The eldest is named Micay. I smile to see Mama playing with her lovely granddaughters. She takes each one of them to my *huaca* for special time alone.

Here is my beautiful sister Chasca's life. She is married to a handsome nobleman, just as she had hoped. There is love in this marriage, and her eyes sparkle with happiness.

I travel to the time of the rains. They fall in abundance, and the people dance and sing praises to the Marked Girl who spoke with the spirit world on their behalf and brought a time of abundance. I visit with the corn kernels planted deep within Pachamama's body as they eagerly stretch out their first roots. I watch as the people feast on the plentiful crops and go to sleep at night with full bellies and minds free of worry.

As the wind, I visit my animal friends. The Mother Jaguar welcomes me to her cave home, and I play with her children. They remember me and are happy I have come to visit. I join Sumac in flight. The Handsome One seems to know I am there with him and calls out in delight. It is just as wonderful as when I was a young girl and visited Beyond for the first time.

I journey backwards and watch myself living the early days of my life. There is Beautiful Round Face, me as a young girl, sitting on Mama's lap giggling. Mama kisses and kisses and kisses me as I offer her a smile as bright as Inti rising in the morning.

I move forward in time and watch the Mother Jaguar attacking me to protect her children. It is a horrifying scene of fear and blood and screams. It is no wonder my younger self chose to forget something so terrifying.

And now I see my scarred self hiding throughout many, many years. I wish I could tell this girl that all will be fine; the suffering will have meaning and be worthwhile. But as the wind, all I can do is watch and learn.

There is my first visit to the Paqo's *wasi*, when his flute music called to me and I dared to enter his home.

I chuckle, watching myself stumble over my own feet as I rush outside, a look of terror twisting my face. No wonder my teacher laughed at me that day.

Here I watch Mama in her kitchen, preparing the evening meal. She hums her usual soothing tune, waiting for the water to boil. I watch in wonder as she purposely places the side of her hand within the bubbling water, a look of resolve on her face. Not once does she cry out. Her determined walk to the Paqo's *wasi*, protecting her burnt hand from the winds with her cloak as she steps along the path, is one of a mother who will do whatever she needs to do for her child. Her face dares anyone who might see her to question her actions.

I am Beyond, but I can feel my body calling me back to the Acllahuasi. It is telling me that there is much to do. The people need more rain, and it is time to begin my journey as a powerful priestess so I may help them. But there is one more time and place that calls to my wind self. It was a favorite of mine back when I was the Ugly One. Come and visit it with me as the wind.

We are home in the *llaqta*. It is night, sometime after Ucho returned from Machu Picchu and the crops grew from the plentiful rains. The people are gathered about the fire, their bellies full and content. Uncle Turu stands in front of the popping flames, waiting in stillness for the tension to build, and I hover on the edge of the crowd, as I used to do. It is a new one, this story Uncle Turu is about to tell.

As the wind, I know that Uncle Turu's long silences before he begins aren't just to create tension. It is his habit to go over the story in his mind, to recall how he wants to tell it. Now he is thinking about the ending of the story he is going to share, as it is still new to him and he wants to tell it right and true. Let us visit Uncle Turu's thoughts and hear how he practices this ending in his mind as the people wait by the fire.

And so the Marked Girl stepped up to the Sacred Rock and placed her scarred cheek against its body. Here Uncle Turu imagines that he will turn his head and lean in, as if touching the side of his face to a large rock. *The Marked Girl spoke with the spirits and asked for the rains. A mighty clap of thunder foretold the end of the dry times as the skies opened and gave the earth its water. The crops grew and the people feasted, always giving praise to the Marked Girl. She had saved her people, right and true.*

Uncle Turu looks at the faces flickering in the light of the flames and offers a smile. It is a story filled with joy and pride that he is about to tell. He is ready. He opens his mouth and begins. Let us whisper along with him, "Ñawpa pachapi, once upon a time . . ."

GLOSSARY

· · · · · · · · · · · · · ·

Quechua was the *runa simi*, the human tongue, of the Incan people. They did not have a written language, and there's no way of knowing exactly how their words were pronounced. But a version of Quechua is spoken today in parts of what used to be the Incan empire, and I have based the pronunciation guide on that.

aca (**uh**-kuh): maize beer

antara (un-**tuh**-ruh): a musical instrument made of wooden pipes bound together

ari (uh-**ree**): yes

aymaran (eye-**muh**-run): a dance that originated in the Aymaran culture and was adopted by the Incan culture

campu (**kuhm**-poo): a pendant

Capac Raymi (**kay**-pack **ray**-me): Magnificent Festival

Chasca (**chuh**-skuh): Morning Star

chasqui (**chuh**-skee): a runner, a messenger

cocha (**koh**-chuh): a high mountain lake

conkana (kon-**kuh**-nuh): a board game using wooden dice and colored bean counters curacas (koo-**ruh**-cuhs): inspectors sent by the Sapa Inca to take an annual census

Cuzco (**koo**-scoh): Center of the World, or navel; the capital city of the Incan empire, now part of Peru

hailli (**hayl**-yee): victory

hanaq (**huh**-nuk): Beyond

huaca (**hwa**-cuh): a spirit rock

Huayna Picchu (**hway**-nuh **pee**-choo): Young Peak

ichu (**ee**-choo): a gray-green grass found at higher altitudes

Illapa (eel-**yuh**-puh): god of thunder and lightning

Inti (**in**-tee): Sun Father, sun god

Inti Raymi (**in**-tee **ray**-me): Festival of the Sun

kachitu (kuh-**chee**-too): beauty

kallpa (**kull**-ypuh): strength

koka (**koh**-kuh): leaves or plant used for tea and for medicinal and ceremonial purposes

llaqta (**lyuhk**-tuh): a village

maca-maca (**muh**-kuh **muh**-kuh): a plant native to the high Andes

Machu Picchu (**ma**-choo **pee**-choo): Old Peak

Mama Killa (**mah**-muh **keel**-yuh): Moon Mother, moon goddess

Mama Ocllo (**mah**-muh **awk**-low): Daughter of the Moon

manca (**muhn**-kuh): a cooking pot

Manco Capac (**muhn**-koh **kay**-pack): Son of the Sun

Micay (**mih**-kay): Beautiful Round Face

Millay (**mihl**-yay): Ugly One

molle (**mol**-yeh): a type of tree

muña (**moon**-yuh): a grass whose scent was used to help with head and stomach problems

munca (**moon**-kuh): a purple flower

musqukuti (moo-skoo-**koo**-tee): dreamtime

Musuq Simi (**moo**-sook **sim**-ee): New Voice

ñawpa pachapi (**nyuh**-puh puh-**chu**-pee): once upon a time

Pachamama (puh-chuh-**mah**-muh): Earth Mother, time

pachis (**puh**-chees): thank you

Paqo (**puh**-koh): Shaman

punga-punga (**poon**-guh **poon**-guh): a flower that was often dried for medicinal purposes

qanimpa (kuhn-**eem**-puh): the past

quena quena (**keh**-nuh **keh**-nuh): a traditional wooden flute

quipu (**kee**-poo): colored thread or strings used to record important information

quwis (kwees): guinea pigs raised indoors for food

Sapa Inca (**suh**-puh **ing**-kuh): Emperor

simi (**sim**-ee): voice or language

Sumac Huanacauri (**soo**-muhk hwuh-nuh-**kaw**-ree): Handsome Rainbow

taccla (**tuhk**-luh): a foot plow

tampu (**tuhm**-poo): rest house

taskikaru (tuh-skee-**kuh**-roo): journey

tumi (**too**-mee): a ceremonial knife often used in sacrifices

Turu (**too**-roo): Bull

Ucho (**oo**-choh): Hot Pepper

vicuña (vih-**coo**-nyuh): a close relative of the alpaca and llama

wasi (**wuh**-see): home

Willka Rumi (**will**-ykuh **room**-ee): Sacred Rock

Wiñay Wayna (**win**-ee **way**-nuh): Forever Young

yachachisqa (yu-chuh-**chee**-skuh): an apprentice

yanapa (yuh-**nuh**-puh): helping

yunka (**yoon**-kuh): the jungle

yuraq sara (**yoo**-ruhk **suh**-ruh): white corn

yuya (**yoo**-yuh): remembering

AUTHOR'S NOTE

I have always loved traveling, and over the years I've visited many places around the world. Peru, with its lush rainforest and mountainous hiking trails, had long called to me, and finally I was able to go. My agenda was simple: to explore and experience a country very different from my own. One highlight of the trip was having a scarlet macaw land right on my head at a nature reserve in the rainforest. Another was visiting Machu Picchu, a magical, ancient city built high in the mountains. I wandered the maze-like passages of the ruins and imagined what it might have been like to walk there when it was a thriving, alive place.

When I returned home, all sorts of unique souvenirs came back with me: beautiful sweaters woven from alpaca wool, *antara* flutes, small rocks and pottery shards I had collected as I hiked through the Andes Mountains, and, of course, many lovely pictures and memories. What I didn't know was that something *else* had come back with me too. A story.

I was trying to finish a novel that I had been working on before my time in Peru. One day I opened my notebook to jot down a few ideas, and suddenly the sentence *I had always been ugly, as far back as I could remember* was staring up at me from the previously empty page. Where in the world had these words come from? Who was saying them? I tried to ignore this unexpected character, but she was insistent. I drew a picture of her, and there she was, one side of her face hidden by a macaw that perched on her shoulder. Her uncovered eye stared at me hauntingly. I knew I had to write her story, and eventually I knew her name: Micay.

I returned to Peru a few years later to research the Incan culture in more detail. Along the Incan trail, I met a modern-day shaman. For many hours, late into the night, I interviewed him as we sipped coca tea by the fire, surrounded by the towering Andes Mountains. He shared the white corn myth with me that night, a story that became part of this book. I also visited Machu Picchu again and imagined it coming back to life. We call it Machu Picchu now, because that is the name of the mountain upon which the city is built, but I wondered what it had been called by the Incans of long ago. For my story, I chose the name Sacred Sun City, but to this day we don't know the true name or exact purpose of this mysterious place.

I stayed in Machu Picchu well past sunset, gazing up at the sky. The stars were nothing like the faint, distant lights I had seen all my life. At that high altitude, they were more like close friends twinkling in the dark space created by the mountains that soared into the hushed air. It was clear that the people who built this place were deeply connected to the sky, the rocks, and the gods they believed dwelled within all. Every stone was shaped and placed with great care, and one towering rock was expertly carved to resemble the mountain behind it. There was no denying the power it commanded in this special, now silent city. It became the Sacred Rock of my story.

In the years that followed, I slowly finished the book, writing and rewriting, trying to remain true to what I had learned of the Inca people as I wove Micay's story into the fabric of their rich culture and spirit. I hope I have done the Incans justice and that Micay is pleased that her story has finally been told.

RESOURCES

· · · · · · · · · · · · · · · · · ·

BOOKS
Nonfiction Books About Machu Picchu

Kops, Deborah. *Machu Picchu: Unearthing Ancient Worlds.* Minneapolis: Twenty-First Century Books, 2009.

Lewin, Ted. *Lost City: The Discovery of Machu Picchu.* New York: Philomel Books, 2003.

Nonfiction Books About the Incas

Calvert, Patricia. *The Ancient Inca.* New York: Franklin Watts of Scholastic, Inc. 2004.

Drew, David. *Inca Life.* Hauppauge, New York: Barron's Educational Series, Inc., 2000.

Newman, Sandra. *The Inca Empire.* New York: Scholastic, Inc., 2010.

Roza, Greg. *Incan Mythology and Other Myths of the Andes.* New York: Rosen Publishing Group, Inc., 2008.

Sayer, Chloe. *The Incan Empire.* New York: Gareth Stevens Publishing, 2011.

Incan Folktale Picture Books and Collections

Garcia, Anamarie, illus. by Janice Skivington. *The Girl from the Sky: An Inca Folktale from South America.* Chicago: Children's Press, 1992.

Jendresen, Erik, and Alberto Villoldo, illus. by Yoshi. *The First Story Ever Told*. New York: Simon & Schuster, 1996.

Kurtz, Jane, illus. by David Frampton. *Miro in the Kingdom of the Sun*. New York: Houghton Mifflin, 1996.

Sepehri, Sandy, illus. by Brian Demeter. *Munay and the Magic Lake: Based on an Incan Tale*. Vero Beach, Florida: Rourke Publishing, 2007.

Novels About the Inca

Clark, Ann Nolan. *Secret of the Andes*. New York: Penguin Books, 1952.

Van de Grier, Susan, illus. by Mary Jane Gerber. *A Gift for Ampato*. Ontario: Groundwood Books, 1999.

WEBSITES

Websites About the Incan Empire

42explore2.com/inca.htm

Links to websites about the Incas, including sites developed by kids for kids.

incas.mrdonn.org/index.html

A website with links to articles about everything from the geography of the Inca Empire to llama legends to Inca roads and bridges. Play games or take a virtual tour of the Inca trail.

kids.nationalgeographic.com/kids/games/
geographygames/brainteaserinca

Test how much you know about the Inca Empire with this interactive game.

kidsblogs.nationalgeographic.com/2009/07/13/
mckenna-on-the-inca-trail-and-the-sun-gate
A blog about hiking to the sun gate, the entrance to
Machu Picchu, written from the point of view of students
traveling in Peru.

pbs.org/wgbh/nova/ancient/lost-inca-empire.html
Information on the lost Inca Empire.

Website About Modern-Day Inca
incas.org
Information about and photos of modern-day Inca people.

Websites About Machu Picchu
docbert.org/MP
A single view of Machu Picchu that allows you to zoom in
and out and move around the complete archaeological site.

machupicchu360.travel
360-degree interactive views of Machu Picchu.

pbs.org/wgbh/nova/ancient/ghosts-machu-picchu.html
A description and link to "Ghosts of Machu Picchu," a fifty-
minute PBS *Nova* video.

whc.unesco.org/en/list/274
Information and photos of Machu Picchu, with links to
other websites.

Websites About the Quechua Language
andes.org/q_index.html
Basic Quechua language lessons in vocabulary, grammar,
and common phrases and dialogue.

freelang.net/online/quechua_cuzco.php?lg=gb
A Quechua-to-English and English-to-Quechua translator.

quechua.org.uk
Information about the Quechua language, including recordings for pronunciation.

MUSIC
CDs

Inkuyo. *Land of the Incas: Music of the Andes.* Fortuna Records, 1991.

Malki, Yurac. *Traditional Music of the Incas.* Legacy International, 1995.

Sulca, Ayllu. *Music of the Incas: Andean Harp & Violin Music from Ayacucho.* Lyrichord Discs Inc., 1992.

Website
andes.org/songs.html
Traditional songs in Quechua translated into English and Spanish. Includes videos of the songs being performed and free music downloads.